"WAIT!"

Something—a sixth sense or simply some sound or hint of movement—made Longarm stiffen and cry out to the girl as she pulled the shed door open.

He was too late. A blur of motion sped out of the interior of the shed toward Alex and a feathered arrow shaft appeared on the front of her duster.

The girl cried out and fainted, toppling over backward into the dirt of the alley. Longarm sprang forward, his Colt in his fist. . . .

Also in the LONGARM series from Jove

LONGARM
LONGARM AND THE LONE STAR LEGEND
LONGARM AND THE LONE STAR VENGEANCE
LONGARM AND THE LONE STAR BOUNTY
LONGARM AND THE LONE STAR DELIVERANCE
LONGARM IN THE TEXAS PANHANDLE
LONGARM AND THE RANCHER'S SHOWDOWN
LONGARM ON THE INLAND PASSAGE
LONGARM IN THE RUBY RANGE COUNTRY
LONGARM AND THE GREAT CATTLE KILL
LONGARM AND THE CROOKED RAILMAN
LONGARM ON THE SIWASH TRAIL
LONGARM AND THE RUNAWAY THIEVES
LONGARM AND THE ESCAPE ARTIST
LONGARM AND THE BONE SKINNERS
LONGARM AND THE MEXICAN LINE-UP
LONGARM AND THE LONE STAR MISSION
LONGARM AND THE TRAIL DRIVE SHAM
LONGARM ON DEATH MOUNTAIN
LONGARM AND THE COTTONWOOD CURSE
LONGARM AND THE DESPERATE MANHUNT
LONGARM AND THE ROCKY MOUNTAIN CHASE
LONGARM ON THE OVERLAND TRAIL
LONGARM AND THE BIG POSSE
LONGARM ON DEADMAN'S TRAIL
LONGARM IN THE BIG BASIN
LONGARM AND THE BLOOD HARVEST
LONGARM AND THE BLOODY TRACKDOWN
LONGARM AND THE HANGMAN'S VENGEANCE
LONGARM ON THE THUNDERBIRD RUN
LONGARM AND THE UTAH KILLERS
LONGARM IN THE BIG BURNOUT
LONGARM AND THE TREACHEROUS TRIAL
LONGARM AND THE NEW MEXICO SHOOT-OUT
LONGARM AND THE LONE STAR FRAME
LONGARM AND THE RENEGADE SERGEANT
LONGARM IN THE SIERRA MADRES
LONGARM AND THE MEDICINE WOLF
LONGARM AND THE INDIAN RAIDERS
LONGARM IN A DESERT SHOWDOWN
LONGARM AND THE MAD DOG KILLER
LONGARM AND THE HANGMAN'S NOOSE
LONGARM AND THE OUTLAW SHERIFF
LONGARM AND THE DAY OF DEATH
LONGARM AND THE REBEL KILLERS
LONGARM AND THE HANGMAN'S LIST
LONGARM IN THE CLEARWATERS
LONGARM AND THE REDWOOD RAIDERS
LONGARM AND THE DEADLY JAILBREAK
LONGARM AND THE PAWNEE KID
LONGARM AND THE DEVIL'S STAGECOACH
LONGARM AND THE WYOMING BLOODBATH
LONGARM IN THE RED DESERT
LONGARM AND THE CROOKED MARSHAL

TABOR EVANS

LONGARM
AND THE TEXAS RANGERS

JOVE BOOKS, NEW YORK

LONGARM AND THE TEXAS RANGERS

A Jove Book / published by arrangement with
the author

PRINTING HISTORY
Jove edition / July 1990

All rights reserved.
Copyright © 1990 by Jove Publications, Inc.
This book may not be reproduced in whole or in part,
by mimeograph or any other means, without permission.
For information address: The Berkley Publishing Group,
200 Madison Avenue, New York, New York 10016.

ISBN: 0-515-10352-7

Jove Books are published by The Berkley Publishing Group,
200 Madison Avenue, New York, New York 10016.
The name ''Jove'' and the ''J'' logo
are trademarks belonging to Jove Publications, Inc.

PRINTED IN THE UNITED STATES OF AMERICA

10 9 8 7 6 5 4 3 2 1

Chapter 1

Longarm came in whistling a sprightly tune. And why not? He was at peace with the world, and it seemed to be at peace with him too, for a change. His belly was full, his balls were empty after an early morning romp with an immodest maiden, and it was a fine, fair, spring day outside the Federal Building on Denver's Colfax Avenue. No way a man could not be feeling good with all that going for him.

Besides, he was not only on time for work this morning, he was several minutes ahead of the official starting time for duty in the United States marshal's office. Marshal Billy Vail was going to be purely shocked.

Longarm quit whistling long enough to greet Marshal Vail's clerk, Henry, who must have been in the habit of starting work sometime in the neighborhood of daybreak. At least Deputy Custis Long never managed to get to work ahead of punctilious and sometimes prissy Henry. Didn't want to, for that matter.

"A great big howdy to you, Henry my man," Longarm said cheerfully. He removed his hat and gave it a flip toward the coatrack in the corner. The low-crowned, snuff-brown Stetson spun through the air like it was floating and landed nicely on an empty hook.

But then, what else could be expected on a day so fine.

Henry scowled. Sometimes Longarm thought the bespectacled little man had no sense of fun.

"What's the matter, Henry? Drip some gravy on my vest or something?" He struck a pose for Henry's benefit and presented himself for inspection.

Henry might not be impressed, but a lady now and then seemed to be.

Even without his hat, Longarm stood well over six feet tall. He had broad shoulders and a horseman's narrow hips. He wore a brown tweed coat, a calfskin vest over a tan flannel shirt, and dark brown corduroy trousers stuffed inside black stovepipe boots. A double-action Colt revolver rode in a cross-draw rig just to the left of his belt buckle, and there was a watch chain draped across the front of his vest. Longarm's face was lean and tanned, more rugged than classically handsome, although the ladies never seemed to gag much when they looked at him. He had brown hair and a thick sweep of brown mustache to match it. Regardless of what he looked like though, this morning Longarm *felt* good. His humor just couldn't have been a whole lot better than this. For a change.

"Well?" he demanded.

Henry ignored the obvious request for compliments and got straight to business. "The marshal wants to see you, Deputy."

"That's what I'm here for," Longarm said cheerily. He turned and started toward the closed door that led to the marshal's private office.

"Huh-uh," Henry said.

"Say what? I thought you told me . . ."

"Not there."

Longarm lifted an eyebrow. "The boss been moved to a new office or something while I wasn't looking?" Billy Vail was *always* available inside that office at this time of day.

And a fair good many nights too, for that matter. The man practically lived at, and for, his work.

"Marshal Vail did not come in to the office this morning," Henry said primly, and with a poorly hidden note of disapproval in his tone. That, Longarm decided, was what had Henry's knickers in a knot this morning and why he wasn't feeling playful.

"Billy? Playing hooky? Cut to the punchline so I can laugh too, Henry."

"He isn't in there, Deputy. He sent a messenger. Quite early too. The boy was waiting here when I arrived." Henry sniffed and reached for a scrap of paper on the always tidy desk before him. Not that he would need to refresh his memory from it, Longarm knew. Henry never forgot anything. Not when it came to business. Henry might forget to make sure he was wearing socks that matched, but he wouldn't ever forget a message.

"He says he wants you to meet him at the Parthenon." This time Henry didn't even try to keep the disapproval out of his voice. He followed the words, in fact, with a grimace and a sniff.

Longarm's reaction was to grin. "On a toot, huh?"

Henry sniffed again but did not otherwise rise to the bait. Both of them knew good and well that the Parthenon was a saloon, albeit a high-class one. Longarm knew the place fairly well. He doubted Henry ever would have had the experience, and wouldn't have let himself enjoy it even if he had.

Longarm had to agree, though, that the Parthenon was one damned unlikely place to be finding Billy Vail before the start of a working day.

"Tell you what, Henry. If the boss is drunk and has the blind staggers, I'll dry him out and pour some coffee into him till he's fit to be seen in polite company."

Henry frowned.

"And if he ain't," Longarm added pleasantly, "I'll tell him that you disapprove of him conducting official business in that wicked, sinful place. That make you happy, Henry?"

"You wouldn't do that, would you?" Henry said, somewhat too quickly. He sounded more worried than ever now.

"Course I would," Longarm said happily. There weren't so many opportunities for a fella to tweak Henry's nose that Longarm wanted to pass one up if or when it was presented. "If you like, I can tell him you say he better get his ass back here where he belongs."

"Longarm!"

The tall deputy laughed and retrieved his Stetson from the coatrack.

"Any messages for Billy, Henry? Once I have him sobered up, that is?"

"Just . . . do what you're told, Deputy."

"Yeah, I expect I will, Henry. I do expect that I will."

Longarm settled his hat in place and ambled out into the hallway, then moved down the corridor to the stone steps outside the Federal Building.

The day was still fine and Longarm's mood still as bright as the sunshine. He set out briskly down the sidewalk. It was only a few minutes' walk to the Parthenon.

Chapter 2

There were only two customers standing at the bar in the dark, cool interior of the Parthenon. Both of them were handsomely dressed gentlemen with silver-gray hair, large bellies and red-veined noses. Drunks of the highest possible class.

Neither of them happened to be United States Marshal Billy Vail.

Longarm made his way through the maze of empty tables to the end of the polished mahogany bar. That was easy to do in a fancy place like this one. The slop joints over by the stockyards might pack their floors with tables so that a man had to wiggle his way between them, but the Parthenon gave its customers elbow room, as well as real gold on the gilt frames around the naked-lady pictures. The place was dandy, all right. Plenty of brass and velvet and gleaming wood. It was nice, really, although Longarm couldn't personally see that a beer or a shot tasted twice as good here as it did anyplace else, even if you paid twice as much for the pleasure of enjoying the same.

"Yes, sir?" the barman said. The fellow hadn't been on duty here all night, that was for sure. He was fresh shaved, and his shirt and collar were crisp.

"I'm looking for Marshal William Vail."

"Yes, sir. This way." The bartender left his early morning drinkers to shake and wheeze by themselves for a moment and led Longarm back to one of the small and very private rooms that lent the Parthenon much of its popularity. The private party areas, and the waiters who pretended deafness when serving them, were particularly favored by the politicians who flocked into the state capital like lemmings rushing toward the sea.

"Thanks." The bartender discreetly disappeared, and Longarm tapped on the door.

"Who is it?"

"Just me, Billy."

"All right."

Longarm tried the doorknob but had to wait a moment until he heard a bolt being withdrawn before he could enter the small chamber with its teardrop chandelier and matching wall sconces. There was a baize-covered table with four chairs around it in the center of the room and a soft, leather-upholstered sofa off to the side. The sofa was big enough that a man—or a real friendly couple—could use it as a bed. And leather wipes off easy without leaving stains behind.

At the moment, though, there wasn't any buxom and powdered lady occupying the sofa. There was a man stretched out on it. Nobody Longarm had ever seen before. Billy Vail was the one who'd opened the door for Longarm. His friend, or guest or whatever, hadn't so much as looked up as far as Longarm could tell.

"Come in, Deputy." This was official business then. Billy calling him by title instead of name told Longarm that much.

Longarm waited while Billy glanced outside to make sure there wasn't anyone hanging around close enough to listen at the walls, then closed and carefully bolted the door again.

This was kinda interesting, Longarm decided.

Billy Vail sure wasn't drunk now or coming off a drunk, but the portly, balding marshal hadn't gotten himself a full night's sleep either. Billy's shirt was rumpled and his collar limp. His eyes were red-rimmed with fatigue, and he hadn't shaved yet this morning. He looked like he'd been up most of the night. On the card table in the center of the room there was a coffeepot—no beer or whiskey glasses though, and there was no smell of liquor in the place—and the congealed remains of a bacon and egg breakfast. Longarm hadn't known the Parthenon served food. Or maybe the meal had been carried in from someplace else.

"Thank you for coming, Deputy."

Thank you? For doing what he was ordered to do? Longarm kept his mouth shut.

"Billy," Billy said.

Longarm blinked.

The man on the sofa sat up, then stood.

The stranger looked to be every bit as tired and dragged out as Billy Vail.

He was a stocky man of middling height, call it five eight, and two hundred pounds, but damned little of that in fat, and was probably somewhere in his fifties. He wore a suit that was of good quality and would have looked just fine with a little attention from a dry cleaner, but at the moment his vest was unbuttoned and the collar on his shirt flapped loose.

He was still wearing his coat. There was a telltale bulge on the left side of his chest that said he wasn't covering just his armpit with that coat.

There was something about the man that suggested twenty years ago he would have been a handful.

"Billy, I'd like you to meet Deputy Custis Long, mostly known as Longarm. Longarm, this is William Mann. Once upon a time known as Billy Two. I, uh, believe you've heard me mention him."

"Well, shit," Longarm said with a quick grin. He removed his hat and offered Billy Two a hand practically in the same motion. "It's a real pleasure to meet you, Mr. Mann." He was still grinning.

Heard Billy mention Billy Two? Shit, he reckoned he had. Plenty.

Billy Two was one of Billy Vail's old partners from Billy's—both Billys'—days in the Texas Rangers. The two Billys had been members of the same Ranger company, and from the way Billy Vail talked now, they shared a hell of a lot more than just duty assignments.

Billy Vail credited Billy Two—a nickname put on him by other members of Captain Big Foot Johnson's company to avoid confusion when orders were being shouted—with saving his skin more than once. He never particularly mentioned any of the times he might have saved Billy Two's neck, but Longarm knew from other sources and more than a bit of personal experience that Billy Vail'd had plenty of salt in him too when he was rambling around out in the field with a badge on his shirt and a gun close to his hand.

"A real pleasure," Longarm repeated, pumping Billy Two's hand.

"Billy One tells me nice things about you too, Deputy," Mann said.

"Yeah, but he lies a lot."

"I hope not," Mann said seriously.

"This, uh, ain't exactly a happy reunion kind of wingding," Longarm observed.

Mann shook his head sadly and turned back toward the sofa where he'd been resting when Longarm came in. His shoulders were slumped, and there was a gray depression tugging at his jowls.

"Longarm," Billy Vail said softly—Billy One in this room, although it was a side of the nicknames that he hadn't ever admitted to before—as he motioned Longarm toward a seat at the table, "someone is trying to frame Billy Two on federal charges of fraud and murder. Federal charges, Longarm. He is . . . he's a fugitive, dammit. And I'm supposed to arrest him. And help them hang him."

Billy's voice was softer than ever now. There was an undertone in it that was desperate. Pleading.

"I want you to help me, Longarm. Help Billy Two, that is. I want you to . . . help me clear Billy's name."

Longarm glanced over toward the sofa. Billy Mann sat there with his head hanging, unwilling to meet his old friend's eyes at this moment.

"And I don't . . . I just *can't* put him in irons, Longarm, and make him sit in a cell while you find the proof of the frame. I just . . . not Billy Two. I can't do it, Longarm."

Longarm blinked again.

Billy *Vail* was telling him this? A fugitive from federal warrants, regardless of how those warrants came to be signed, was sitting here in front of the United States marshal, and Billy Vail didn't want his deputy to make the arrest?

Longarm took in a deep breath, glanced once more from Billy Two to Billy One. Then he puffed his cheeks out and very slowly exhaled. "Tell me about it," he said.

Chapter 3

This was one ticklish son of a bitch of a deal, Longarm realized when Billy Vail was done with his part of the talking.

He leaned forward and helped himself to a cup of coffee from the pot. It was getting cold by now. He made a face and pushed it aside, settling for a cheroot instead. He took his time about trimming and lighting the smoke. He wanted a few moments to think.

Billy Vail, of course, had had most of the night to do his thinking. And come to his decisions. Longarm was taking it on all at once here.

The basic facts of it were simple enough.

William T. Mann, Billy Two to Billy Vail, was a fugitive from federal charges of murder and fraud. The alleged crimes had taken place in the federally administered strip known as No-Man's-Land that lay between the top of the Texas panhandle and the southern border of Colorado. Texas and the then Territory of Colorado were originally supposed to connect. But when the survey was made, under threat of

Indian attack from several different tribes, the survey party made a "small" error of forty miles or thereabouts running across the top of the Texas panhandle.

When the mistake was finally discovered, the government decided it was easier to keep the unappropriated land and administer it as part of an adjacent tract to the east. This tract along with the adjoining strip comprised the Indian Nations, several reservations assigned to less civilized Indian nations and assorted other parcels of government-owned or government-run property.

No-Man's-Land had become a haven for men on the run, for squatters wanting free land and for assorted confidence artists and scammers. It was, after all, a hell of a long way from Fort Smith, Arkansas, and the federal marshals who rode out of there.

Fort Smith had responsibility for No-Man's-Land, though, and Billy Vail's Denver office wouldn't normally much give a shit what happened there. Or hear right away about the warrants outstanding down that way, which was why this whole situation had snuck up on Billy Vail and put him in such a whirl now.

The way Billy Two explained it, his troubles started with a real-estate scam in No-Man's-Land.

"Like yours, Billy One, my name is not unremembered in Texas. Maybe that's why the scoundrel chose to use my name when he planned his fraud. At least that's the only reason I can think of. He represented himself as me, damn him, and he preyed upon people who remembered my service to Texas in the Rangers and felt reassured by my alleged participation in the town development.

"The town site, you see, was supposed to be in Texas. It was widely advertised as a new town site, and information was distributed that a rail spur running more or less along the old Cimarron Cutoff of the Santa Fe Trail would be announced soon. This bogus town site was supposed to be on the new railroad right-of-way, so early settlers would have the advantage of an immediate leap in property values just as soon as the announcement was made.

"The town was laid out and plotted, and there was extensive advertising in the East. Buyers poured in from Vermont, New Hampshire, places like that. I've seen some of the ads myself. It promises rich farmland. Now I ask you: Farmland? In No-Man's-Land? Why, the only crop a man could raise in that country is dust. With a little rock thrown in. But the ads were persuasive. They promised an abundance of fine water just under the surface, easily reached by springpole drill rigs and readily drawn by patent wind-powered mills."

Mann grimaced. "They tell me that even people who came to inspect the town site often swallowed this line of bull and paid over good money for town lots, even when they could see with their own eyes that there wasn't anything there and likely never will be. These sons of bitches even contracted to sell them the windmills, damn them, then naturally disappeared without the first mill ever having been delivered or the first well dug.

"And the leader of them was using *my* name to do his dirty work, damn him. Pretending to have been a former Ranger himself so these poor, gullible people would accept and trust him." Billy Two shook his head.

"Anyway," he went on, "apparently quite a few of the lots were sold and the money paid over. I don't know the details, of course, because I wasn't there at the time and had never heard of this so-called town of Oak Creek." He fixed Billy Vail with a baleful look. "Oak Creek? There isn't an oak within two hundred miles of the place. A come-on, obviously, to make absent investors think the land was watered and lush. But it worked. For all I know they might have sold the same lots by mail *and* to settlers who had come to inspect before they bought.

"And of course it is a federal offense to fraudulently buy or sell untitled federal lands. That alone should be enough to land them all in prison. That is where the fraud charges come from."

"What about the murder?" Longarm injected.

"I'm coming to that. The scheme couldn't go on forever,

of course. Although apparently these scoundrels thought it could run a little longer than in fact it did.

"Their mistake came about when one of the new settlers got into a quarrel with another man. Both, apparently, wanted to buy the same corner lot in the phony business district. They argued, and one of them killed the other. No question about that crime, of course. There were competent witnesses to it, and in fact the man who had done the killing was remorseful. He was from someplace in the East and knew very little about guns, certainly never got in a fight before." Mann gave them a rueful smile. "You know how it is with some easterners. They come out here and suddenly think they're ten feet tall and have fangs where their molars used to be. No law at hand, so they'll make their own. We've put cuffs on enough of that kind, haven't we, Billy One?"

Billy Vail nodded.

"And of course there *was* no law in this Oak Creek. Someone asked the Rangers to come in and prosecute the easterner. Manslaughter, it would be. The two men fought in an outburst of passion; there wasn't anything premeditated about it." The former Ranger would certainly know the difference between manslaughter and murder just as well as Longarm and Billy Vail did.

"The Rangers knew nothing about this new town site, it not actually being in Texas like these settlers were told, and when they found it they quite naturally realized that the site was well north of Horse Butte and therefore was part of No-Man's-Land. Not in Texas at all. Just as naturally, they said so. They told the people in Oak Creek that their deeds were not valid and that Texas Rangers had no jurisdiction over any crimes committed there.

"While that was going on at one end of the town, this man who was presenting himself to be me must have somehow gotten word that the game was up. They'd been discovered. Again this is speculation, but apparently he argued with his partners in the fraud. Over a division of the illicitly gotten proceeds, over a woman, we may never know what

13

it was they fought about. In short, this man who claimed to be former Ranger William Mann murdered both his partners and fled.

"The Rangers couldn't pursue him, because there was no crime committed in their jurisdiction. They had no charges against him. They did, however, hurry to the nearest telegraph and get a wire off to Fort Smith informing the federal marshal there about the crimes and about the existence of this Oak Creek. Warrants were immediately secured, against me since mine was the name that was misused, and a federal deputy working out of Fort Smith was assigned to the case.

"I heard about it only by chance. Good chance, as it turns out. I was in the Texas panhandle and received word from a friend that I was the subject of a manhunt." Mann shook his head. "I don't know, Billy One. Maybe I should have stayed and tried to face them. But . . . the Fort Smith deputy is not the sort of man one wants to give oneself up to. Not even peaceably. Twenty years ago . . . That doesn't matter now, does it. This isn't twenty years ago. This is now, and my nerve isn't what it used to be, Billy One. I couldn't . . . I couldn't stand being put in irons and thrown into a cell with men who would remember what I used to be. And frankly I have no confidence that the frame-up will be discovered. *If* I were to live long enough to stand trial. I mean, surely by now Oak Creek has disappeared. All the people who were there and who could testify that I am not the man who sold the lots to them are surely gone by now. They will have scattered in a hundred directions. And the prosecutor won't care enough to find them all and drag them to Fort Smith to testify."

"The Rangers can be found easy enough," Longarm said.

"Sure, but the Rangers never saw the man who claimed to be me," Mann said. "All they can testify to is that those men were murdered. *And that I supposedly did it.*"

"Oh."

"You see what I mean? I . . . I guess I panicked. I knew Billy One was a U.S. marshal himself now. I took the first trains to Denver. Got in last night—I suppose it was this morning by then—and dragged him out of bed.''

"You say you don't want to be taken in by the deputy who's been assigned to the case?"

Mann gave his old friend a sad look. Probably didn't want Billy One to think he was scared, Longarm thought. Although he obviously was. "Campbell," he said.

Longarm grunted. That did explain it. Lewis Campbell was one of the deputies riding out of Fort Smith. In a matter of a few short months Campbell had built a reputation for himself. The man was even quicker on the trigger than crazy Dutch, who worked out of Denver. Campbell was solid and dependable. Put him on a case and he would damn sure bring his prisoner in. But damn seldom a prisoner who was alive and breathing. Longarm hadn't ever met the man, but he had heard plenty about him.

If Mann's nerve had failed, no wonder he would not want Lew Campbell to take him into custody.

But not wanting Billy Vail to hold Billy Two in custody ... well, this wasn't an area that Longarm had been invited to mix into.

The fact was, Billy Vail accepted his old partner's concern and sympathized with it. Moreover, Billy Vail was willing to go along with it while Longarm trekked south to No-Man's-Land and tried to do something about finding the man who'd really sold those federal lands and murdered those two other fraud artists.

Billy Vail leaned closer and entered the conversation for the first time since Billy Two started talking.

"I know what you're thinking, Longarm. And I know what I'm asking you to do. I'm asking you to go out on a limb with me. If anyone finds out about this before you have the proof of Billy Two's innocence ... I could lose my badge, and yours might go under too."

Longarm waved that concern aside. It was the least of his worries.

"Frankly, Longarm, I don't even want Henry to know

about this. You know how fussy he is about dotting every *i*."

Yeah, Longarm knew that about Henry. And until today "knew" the same about Billy Vail too. How many times had Billy Vail reamed Custis Long over some minor bending of the rules? Hell, Longarm couldn't begin to count them all. And now . . .

The fact of the matter was, Longarm was in no position here to judge a boss who he admired and respected as much as he did Marshal William Vail. And it was William Vail's ass that had been saved many times over by William Mann. Longarm wasn't in any position to judge Billy Two any more than Billy Vail.

At least they had jurisdiction in the matter. Sort of. The crimes had taken place on federal lands, after all. The offenses were therefore federal. And if it was the Fort Smith and not the Denver office that issued the warrants, well, every federal peace officer has a duty to pursue every federal crime. Right?

Close enough for Longarm's purposes.

"We do have one other problem," Billy Vail was saying. "I need a place where Billy Two can, uh, hole up. So to speak. He can't be out in the open here. I would ask Billy Two to stay with me, but, well, my wife isn't fond of remembering the old days when I was out in the field. I know she'd complain to some of her friends about Billy Two being here, and that could send the whole thing up. We're sure to get copies of those Arkansas warrants in the next day or two. And I certainly don't want the whole office to know about this. Just you, Longarm."

It was, come to think of it, a high compliment to Deputy Custis Long that Marshal Vail had chosen to let him in on this one. There isn't a higher form of praise than trust. And it was trust that Billy Vail was giving him here.

"I can take care of that too," Longarm said. "No problem. I won't be needing my room while I'm gone, and my landlady isn't nosy. The rent's paid far enough ahead that she won't be coming around for anything. He can stay there without anybody asking questions. By the time I need the room again, hell, you two can come back to the Parthenon and have yourselves a good celebration. Open and loud as you like." Longarm forced a reassuring smile that he didn't much feel. It did seem to make the two Billys feel better, though, and that was the whole idea of it.

Longarm stood and reached for another cheroot. "Mr. Mann, why don't you come with me. There's a few things I want to ask you yet, but we can do that on the way over to my room. Marshal Vail needs to get himself cleaned up and in the office before his clerk has a fit of apoplexy from wondering what's up. No need to cause any more questions than we have to here. Billy, is there any reason why I shouldn't use vouchers for my expenses? It is a federal case, after all."

Vail gnawed on that for a moment. Their jurisdiction was, after all, mighty shaky. In theory, at least, the case was already solved and waiting only for an arrest and prosecution in Fort Smith before the hard-nosed judge there.

"Go ahead, Longarm. Run this one like usual. If there's any problem about it later, I'll pay the vouchers myself."

"Whatever you say, Billy. Mr. Mann, are you ready to go get a look at your temporary home?"

"Yes, it's . . . my fate is in your hands, Deputy." He stood, looking years older than Billy Vail now.

Longarm kinda wished Mann hadn't put it just that way. "I'll leave straight from the rooming house, Billy. That way I don't have to tell Henry no lies. If I have to wire you about anything . . . hell, I'll think of something that won't tip the deal. See you later."

Longarm led William Mann out into a spring day that didn't seem quite so fine and bright now as it had just a little while earlier. He didn't *like* being responsible for Billy Vail's future well-being, damnit. Not even when Billy One wanted him to be.

Chapter 4

There was no decent way to get down to the panhandle country from Denver, much less a direct way.

First Longarm had to take the Denver & Rio Grande south through Raton. Then a Santa Fe—which for reasons of its own did not and never would go to Santa Fe—southwest, even though he needed to go southeast to reach Oak Creek. Then a stagecoach to Santa Rosa. And finally the narrow-gauge Pecos & Pacific Line north and east again to reach Coldwater, Texas. Coldwater, near as Longarm could figure it, was the closest any railroad or telegraph would pass to this mythical Oak Creek place in No-Man's-Land.

A journey that should have taken a day's time if there was any direct and modern way to do it ended up requiring the better part of two days' travel. And by the time Longarm got there he was bleary eyed and out of sorts from having to try to sleep sitting up in an assortment of swaying, rattling, rickety contraptions.

It was late afternoon when he finally stumbled down the

steel steps of the P&PL coach with his bag in one hand and McClellan saddle in the other.

His eyes stung from a nearly constant application of cinders and coal smoke. His scalp felt gritty and layered with filth. He hadn't shaved since his last morning in Denver, and he hadn't had time for a bath since then either. He felt, in short, like shit.

The sight of Coldwater, Texas, did nothing to improve his humor.

The place was an ugly brown lump cast down beside the railroad tracks. A dozen or so sagging, weathered, never-painted buildings. A railroad depot. A forlorn windmill with a small steel water-storage tank at its feet. And far as Longarm could see, that was about all she wrote for Coldwater, Texas.

He wasn't thrilled.

A squint at the sky toward the west where the sun was steadily sinking told him there was no point in trying to hire a horse and start out for Oak Creek until morning. Even if there had been a point to it he just damned well wasn't going to do it. Not without a shave and a bath and a good night's sleep beforehand.

He beckoned the first youngster he saw. "You wouldn't have a hotel in town would you, son?"

"No, sir," the boy said.

Longarm's expression drooped.

"There's a lady takes in roomers, though," the boy offered.

"That's more like it. If you can lead me to it, son, you're hired."

The kid gave him a gap-toothed grin. "Yes, sir. Right this way." He grabbed Longarm's saddle and led the way across the street and a hundred yards or so to the east edge of what town there was. "Right here, mister. That'll be a nickel, please."

"Son, the way I feel right now I figure it's worth a dime."

Longarm retrieved the McClellan from the boy and gave him the coin. Both parties seemed satisfied by the deal.

The rooming house was run by a woman who introduced herself as the Widow Cates. She didn't specify if she was actually widowed or if she was of the grass variety. Longarm could see the sense of it either way. Either her husband must have come to his senses and run off one fine night or else he committed suicide so he wouldn't have to wake up to his missus every morning.

The Widow Cates was probably the ugliest human female Longarm had ever laid eyes on. Hell, maybe the ugliest female anything. Buffalo cows and circus elephants included.

She was fat and flabby and had as much facial hair as a pot-liquor hound, just about. Whatever teeth she might once have had had parted company with her years back, and apparently she'd gotten busy full-time growing warts to compensate for that lack.

None of that mattered in the slightest.

"Ma'am, I need a room in the worst way. And a hot bath and shaving water too."

"Sixty cents if you share the bed, dollar if you want it all to yourself, mister. That includes supper and breakfast, no lunch. Bath is free but the hot water's ten cents extra. Shaving water is free morning or night but not both."

"I'll take it," Longarm said quickly. There wouldn't be much in the way of choices in Coldwater, he suspected. "And the bed all to myself if you please."

"It isn't what I please that matters, just what you want to pay for. In advance."

"I might be using the room for a spell. No way to tell yet. I hope you'll take a government voucher for it."

"Government? About all we see of the government hereabouts is the soldier boys, and them not but once or twice a year."

Longarm introduced himself.

The homely woman smiled, the change of expression softening her features but falling far short of making her handsome. "Then I expect you'll want to meet one of my other boarders, Marshal Long. You can meet him at supper. Amos Vent. He's a Texas Ranger, Amos is. Nice boy. You'll like him."

Longarm's interest quickened. The Ranger being here would be a stroke of good luck if this Vent happened to be one of the boys who was on hand when the Oak Creek swindle was unmasked. "I'll look forward to that, ma'am, though first thing I want to do is get cleaned up."

"Let me show you your room then, Marshal, and where to find the tub. I have water hot in the stove. I'll carry it to you while you get yourself settled." She patted his shoulder in a motherly fashion and led him inside.

Longarm was starting to feel better already just from thinking about that bath and shave.

Chapter 5

Longarm felt at least half human by the time Mrs. Cates announced dinner. He made his way into the dining room and found two other tenants of the rooming house already at their places at the kitchen end of the table. Neither man bothered to introduce himself. They were interested in a conversation that was all their own. Longarm got the impression the men were permanent residents in the place and saw no reason to hobnob with transients like this deputy or the missing Texas Ranger.

Amos Vent made it to the table only seconds before Mrs. Cates began bringing platters of food out of the kitchen. He took a seat at Longarm's end of the table and reached over to shake hands and introduce himself. Longarm returned the favor.

Vent smiled. He seemed genuinely pleased to meet the tall federal officer. "Long, eh? I've heard 'bout you, Deputy. Call you Longarm, don't they?"

"That's right."

"Me, I'm mostly called 'hey you,'" Vent said with a chuckle. "New fella in the company, you see."

Longarm recalled now that the Rangers were set up in an almost military structure. Sometimes they operated in a company-sized force, sometimes in ones or twos out on their own, depending on the circumstances.

"My pleasure," Longarm assured the Ranger.

Despite his explanation that he was the new man in the Ranger company, Vent was a man close to Longarm's age. He was of slight build and not particularly impressive appearance. His features were ordinary and unmemorable, and he gave an impression of youth. Mrs. Cates, Longarm remembered, had called him a boy, even though he had to be in his thirties.

The Rangers had no uniforms, but Private Vent was wearing the outfit that was as near to one as mattered. Dark trousers, high-topped boots with an undershot riding heel, wide-brimmed hat with a tall crown, collarless white shirt buttoned to the throat with a badge pinned to it. And of course the obligatory gun-belt with the holster canted, like Longarm's, for a cross-draw. The outfit wasn't regulation, but nearly every Ranger "chose" to adopt it.

"I thought you was riding out of Denver, Longarm," Vent observed as he reached for a helping of potatoes.

"You thought right." Longarm accepted the bowl from him and plopped a mound of the mashed spuds onto his plate.

"Then how is it you're replacing Deputy Campbell out o' Fort Smith?"

"I'm not."

"Really? I mean... sorry, but I guess I kinda made a wrong turn there someplace. I mean, that's what I'm here for. Supposed t' meet up with this Deputy Campbell an' fill him in on what I know about a situation just north o' the border here." Vent grinned. "It ain't so common for us t' be runnin' inta you federal boys. Reckon I made an assumption. Sorry."

23

"No problem. I'm here investigating complaints about a man, former Ranger in fact, name of William Mann." Longarm decided on the spur of the moment that there was no point in being specific about what those supposed complaints were. Better not to tip anybody that there might be a conflict between his assignment and that of Lew Campbell. "You know him?"

"Now ain't that strange," Vent said. "He's the same fella I'm supposed t' tell Deputy Campbell about. An' to answer your question, Deputy, no, I don't actually know the man. Heard plenty about him, o' course. He used to ride in Captain Johnson's Ranger company. But that was long before my time."

"You say Fort Smith is interested in Mann too?" Longarm acted like it was news to him.

"That's right." Ranger Vent shook his head in wonder and proceeded to give Longarm an account of the dealings at Oak Creek that was very much like the one Longarm had already heard from Billy Two.

Except in Vent's telling there was no room for doubt that the former Ranger had gone bad and committed both fraud and murder in No-Man's-Land.

"We would have given chase ourselves up there except we hadn't no jurisdiction," Vent explained, "an' mostly because there was other need for us down here where we do have a say in things. The sergeant didn't like leaving a hot scent like that, but we had t' get down t' Estacado an' see t' some wire boomers. Otherwise we coulda stayed on him an' brought him in for you."

"Boomers?" Lonngarm asked. It wasn't a term, or a crime, he was familiar with.

"Yeah. Boomers. You know. Guy takes a keg o' powder or some of that newfangled dynamite stuff an' makes a boom. Lotta landowners putting wire up around their pastures. Other fellas don't like it so they hire in these crazy sumbitch boomers t' blow the fence lines. An' sometimes t' blow up other stuff. Like people. Gettin' so half our time is spent chasin' boomers."

"Right. Boomers," Longarm said. "You were one of the Rangers up there in this . . . what'd you say the place was?"

"Oak Creek," Vent supplied. "Yeah, I was with 'em. Sergeant Foster, Private Wilcox, an' me. Then we all went larrupin' down t' Estacado an' caught them boomers. Then Sergeant Foster told me t' come back up here an' wait on this Fort Smith deputy name of Campbell while him an' Wilcox took the prisoners an' the bodies in."

Vent reported all that in a completely matter-of-fact manner, with no hint that there was anything remotely exceptional about there being prisoners and bodies for the tiny Ranger detachment to dispose of after their assignment was completed.

Longarm was beginning to think that new Ranger Amos Vent might not look like much or puff his chest out real big, but that it just could be there was considerable grit residing under that unimposing exterior that Vent showed to the world.

Longarm was also beginning to think that Ranger Vent was a man he could like.

"While you're waiting for Campbell to show, Amos, would you mind showing me where this Oak Creek place was?"

"Glad to, Longarm. Give me somethin' t' do other than set around an' get fat." Vent sounded purely serious about that. But he probably weighed a hundred thirty pounds and hadn't an ounce of fat on him. "An' by the by, there ain't no 'was' to it. Far as I know, the folks as came in an' settled Oak Creek are still there. They feel they bought them a town fair an' square an' they're gonna stick with 'er. Though o' course we already told 'em there wasn't nothing legal about their title claims. Stubborn bunch."

Longarm grunted. He wasn't all that surprised, really. The kind of man who will come to a bare and dusty chunk of dirt and decide that tomorrow that emptiness will become a farm or a town or a ranch has to have some sand in him or he wouldn't be there in the first place.

"We'll leave first light if that's all right with you, Longarm," Vent suggested.

"Fine with me."

"Meantime, why don't I show you the sights of Coldwater." The Ranger grinned. "Such as they are."

"My pleasure, Amos."

The peace officers quit their talking for the moment and dug into the meal Mrs. Cates had prepared. They had to do it fast if they expected there to be anything left for them. The two regulars in the house were acting like they wanted to surround the edibles in a hurry, and they weren't much concerned about what would be left for the interlopers.

Chapter 6

"What I ought to do, Amos, is to punch you in the mouth for waking me so early and then not having the decency to at least pretend to be hung over," Longarm complained.

Ranger Vent laughed. He looked fresh and dewy eyed and acted like he had no idea what a hangover was supposed to feel like. Although as Longarm recalled he had every right to one this morning.

And at five-thirty in the morning too.

"Hell, Longarm, I done let you lay in this long, didn't I?"

"You mean you didn't just crawl out yourself?"

"I been up more'n an hour. Been over t' the yard an' found a good horse for you. Shit, shaved an' shampooed. All that." The little man acted like he was coming off twelve hours of deep sleep instead of a roaring drunk.

Longarm shook his head. Damned Amos could make a man start to feel old before his time. He fingered his chin and decided he didn't need to shave again. He'd done that just before supper last night. He pulled his coat on and reached for his Stetson.

"Gimme your saddle there, Longarm, an' I'll get you fixed up while you visit the backhouse."

"No need for you to do that."

"Aw, I don't mind."

"Mighty kind of you."

By the time Longarm returned to the rooming house, breakfast was ready and Longarm was ready for it. He and Vent and the two regulars ate in silence, and the peace officers told Mrs. Cates good-bye on their way out into the new day.

"Long ride ahead?" Longarm asked.

"Not much. We'll be there in the forenoon." Vent slouched easily into a battered old stock saddle that sat on just about the homeliest old blue roan Longarm had ever seen. Ranger Vent's mount was to horseflesh what the Widow Cates was to womankind. On the other hand, the ugly roan was solidly built beneath its patchy hide.

Longarm took a moment to inspect the cheekstraps on his bridle and slide a finger under the cinch of his McClellan. Vent had secured everything just the way Longarm would have done it himself, and the rented horse had been chosen for its soundness and not its looks. Amos knew his business, all right. Longarm mounted, and Vent led the way north at a slow, road-eating lope.

"That's Horse Butte," Vent said an hour or so later, pointing off to the left. "We calculate the border between us an' No-Man's-Land as bein' along the top of the south face o' the butte there. Had a surveyor tell us we're tryin' t' add five an' a half feet t' the State o' Texas by doin' it that way, but I never heard of a bullet or a Comanche neither one carin' t' figger it quite that fine."

From that point on the men would be riding in Longarm's legal jurisdiction instead of Amos Vent's.

"Be in Oak Creek directly," Amos offered. He reached into a pocket for a chew, declining the cheroot Longarm offered.

"Directly" turned out to be another three hours of travel. They reached Oak Creek by mid-morning.

The new town was, oddly, actually larger than Coldwater, Texas. A score or more of buildings were standing on and around the single main street, most of them built of stone and sod but some of them sturdily constructed of milled lumber. Oak Creek was far from the ghost town Longarm had been led to expect. The squatters who had come here in good faith but bad joss had come expecting to build and to stay.

As they rode in Longarm could see the paddles of four windmills turning lazily in the breeze, drawing the water that the confidence artists who'd pulled this scam had had no way of knowing was there when they proudly told the world about it.

"There's one new mill an' four new buildings since I was up here last," Amos said. "Damn place has actually gotten bigger."

"More buyers showing up to claim their lots," Longarm suggested.

"Ayuh. Damn shame, ain't it."

"Fraud generally is. It's the honest fella who gets hurt by it, not the son of a bitch who's running it."

"Me, I hope Billy Mann gets hurt by it plenty," Amos said. "Quick as you or Campbell finds him. Guy like that give us Rangers a bad name, y'know. Can't say as we like that much."

Longarm grunted. He was going to have to watch himself, though. He didn't want anyone on either side of the state border wondering why a federal officer was wanting to defend the interests of former Texas Ranger William Mann.

The deputy and the Ranger slowed their mounts to a walk as they reached the edge of Oak Creek and rode onto the beaten dirt that served as a street here.

Chapter 7

Ranger Amos Vent seemed to be a popular man in Oak Creek, even if he did lack jurisdiction north of the Texas line. He and Longarm hadn't any more than drawn rein outside the combined hotel and saloon, the only two-story structure in town, than there were half a dozen men out on the boardwalk to greet him and take his horse to the nearest hitch rail. The courtesy was extended to Vent's companion as well.

"Pleased to see you, Amos, pleased to see you," a beefy, florid-faced man said over and over as he pumped the Ranger's hand.

Vent accepted the effusive greeting calmly, then turned to Longarm and said, "This here is Merle Dyche, Longarm. Him and his brother Monroe are the, uh, biggest lot holders in Oak Creek. Merle runs the saloon an' hotel here. Monroe has the mercantile across the street there." Vent opened his mouth to continue, but a smiling Merle Dyche cut him short.

"I'm the mayor too now, Amos," Dyche said proudly. "We organized the town. Just like you told us to do. And we've applied for that post office too." Dyche seemed pleased as punch about his announcements. He winked and added, "Didn't quite remember to mention in the application just precisely where the town is, eh?" He laughed.

Amos Vent squirmed more than a little at that, and Longarm could guess why. The tall deputy had to work at keeping a straight face in light of Amos's discomfort. Amos hadn't gotten around to admitting that he'd been passing out advice to these squatters about how they might go about hanging onto their illegally occupied town site.

"And we've named Monroe as our town marshal, and we've elected us a town council, and now we're in the process of organizing a county commission too," Dyche gushed on, blithely unaware of Amos Vent's growing discomfort. "Everything just like you said, Amos."

The portly, middle-aged saloon keeper and part-time mayor might have run on like that at length, but Ranger Vent was finally able to slow him down with an embarrassed cough and a tug on Dyche's sleeve.

"Merle, I really think you oughta meet this fella here," Amos said. There was considerable red showing under the tan on his neck by now.

"Really? Of course. I'm being rude, aren't I?" Mayor Dyche stepped happily in front of Longarm and extended a plump hand for another round of vigorous shaking. "Always a pleasure to meet any friend of Amos's," he assured Longarm.

"Now I'm real glad to hear that, Mister Mayor," Longarm said. He shook the offered hand.

"Merle, as I was gonna tell you before you, uh, gave me the good news . . . this here is Custis Long. Uh, Deputy United States Marshal Custis Long."

"Oh, shit." Dyche turned loose of Longarm's hand like it had gone suddenly red hot. One of the men standing nearby groaned and gave the mayor a dirty look. A few of the others began shifting away on tiptoes, like they were quite willing to pretend they hadn't been there at all, no sir, not me.

Longarm laughed. He couldn't help it. "Merle, nobody told me to come down here and have anything to do with land or the question of who owns, or doesn't own, just what. 'Less I get some orders to the contrary, I reckon I'll let wiser heads than mine figure that one out. All I'm looking for is information about this fella William Mann."

Dyche breathed a sigh of relief, and the men nearby who had been intent on deserting him quit their drift toward obscurity.

"You're, uh, sure about that, Marshal Long?"

"'Less I find some reason to the contrary." He had a hook into these folks if he should ever need to use it. There was no sense in abandoning the leverage completely, he reasoned, smiling as he did so. "And you can call me Longarm, Merle. All my friends do."

"Whew. Come inside, gentlemen. Randall, would you run across the street and ask Monroe to join us, please?" One of the bystanders nodded and started across the wide patch of dirt that was the main street of Oak Creek.

Merle Dyche led Vent and Longarm inside his saloon to the shaded and cool barroom.

By the middle of the afternoon Longarm had met every one of Oak Creek's leading citizens, and had a fair start on being able to boast of conversations with all the other residents too. At least those who had been on hand when the man who called himself William Mann and his partners, one known as Albert "Tuck" Tucker and the other a Farley Moffat, both now deceased, were conducting their illegal business affairs in the un-town. A good many folks had moved into the area since.

The only amazement to come out of all the talking was that everybody told very much the same story. Witnesses to a crime will generally come up with wild variations on a common theme when they go to recounting who did what to whom. On the other hand, this case wasn't one that involved sudden and unexpected violence of the sort that distorts a man's perceptions. This affair had played out over a period of weeks, even months, and nobody'd been excited or upset while it was going on.

Everyone agreed that William Mann represented himself as former Texas Ranger Billy Mann and boasted often about his exploits with Big Foot Johnson's Ranger company.

Everyone agreed that Land Sales Agent Mann was somewhere in his middle fifties, of average height but something above average weight, seemed to be muscular rather than fat, and preferred nicely tailored suits in a dark broadcloth. None of them, even under Longarm's careful prompting, said they had ever seen this Mann with a firearm. No, they hadn't seen any indication of a holster or concealed weapon.

The one time Longarm had seen the real Billy Two he'd been wearing a shoulder rig that was clearly obvious under the cut of his coat.

Except for that, though, the descriptions these Oak Creek folks gave would fit the real Billy Mann like a glove.

Possibly, Longarm thought, that was why the schemer had chosen Billy Two to pick on when he went and created a false identity with just a little bit of judicious lying. Like Ranger stories and other tales of imaginary exploits.

Come to think of it, Longarm realized, he himself likely would have accepted an impostor's word that he was Billy Two if Billy One hadn't been on hand to vouch for Mann's identity. Hell, anybody would if they didn't have all the facts.

"You keep asking us for details about this Mann fellow, Marshal," one of the bilked townspeople said, "and of course we understand that you're wanting information to go on a Wanted poster for him. The pity is that we can't give you a picture of him. We could've, you see, except for the fire."

Longarm lifted an eyebrow. This was the first anybody'd mentioned a picture or a fire. The man in front of him at the moment was a harness maker and saddler called Mike Rhea. Rhea had been in Oak Creek before all the fatal excitement, but just barely; he'd arrived from Connecticut

33

a matter of days before the scam fell apart. Longarm really hadn't expected to get much out of him.

"You could have given me a picture, you say? What kind of picture?" He shot a glance toward Amos Vent, who was busy whispering something to Merle Dyche. Vent hadn't said anything about pictures.

"Photograph," Rhea said. "There was at least one taken that I can recall."

Longarm's interest quickened. "Tell me about it."

Rhea shrugged. "Didn't seem important at the time. The photograph, I mean. We were having this ceremony, see. Two whole coaches of us had come in. Special coaches laid on for us by the Wakefield Express Company. We all were coming together, see. Most from the New Britain area like me and Emil Jabbs—Emil's given up and gone home now—and Jens Olstead and some of the other boys. Some of the crowd came down from New Hampshire. There'd been a lot of advertising up that way and a sales agent who called on us and talked to us about how fine it was here and how much opportunity there'd be. Anyway, there was this whole bunch of us come in together. Two coachloads of us plus a freight wagon the company sent to haul our things with us. It was quite the occasion, you see, with so many arriving to take up their lots all at the same time.

"Mann and Tucker and this Moffat fellow made a regular ceremony of presenting our deeds to us." Rhea's face twisted with bitterness for a moment. "And taking our money at the same time, you see."

Longarm nodded. The man was entitled to some bitterness over that part of it.

"Anyway, they set up a folding table with bunting on the front, and the three of them sat behind it with their ledgers and papers and blank certificates of title. And we all lined up and marched up to them like sheep to the slaughter. Huh! We didn't even need a Judas goat to follow. We did it to ourselves. Walked up and signed papers and paid over money and walked away with those useless damn deeds in our pockets."

"You were saying something about pictures, though?" Longarm prompted, trying to get the man back on the track.

"Right. The pictures. This table, see, was set up right outside the hotel here."

"It was still under construction," Dyche put in. "We had most of the framing up by then and a false front. It was Tucker, I think, who asked if they could use the false front as a backdrop for the ceremony. Naturally I said I'd be pleased. And it was me who asked the photographer to come take pictures of the affair. I was thinking I could use the prints to advertise the place when I had it completed."

"Hell, Merle, I thought the photographer was Mann's idea," Rhea said.

"No, it was—"

"Gentlemen. Please. Let's keep to the point here. You say there were pictures taken?"

Both men nodded. "That's right," Dyche said. "I had Wilson Maxwell set up his equipment out front so he could get the pictures for me."

"Come to think of it," Rhea injected, "Mann did look uneasy when the camera was brought out. I don't think he ever did look directly at it or sit so it could look directly at him. And he kinda sat with his temple resting on his hand. Like this." The harness maker propped an elbow on the table and demonstrated, the effect of it hiding much of his face from view.

"You're right, Mike. I never thought about that before, but he could've wanted to avoid having his picture took but didn't want to come out and say so."

"Didn't want to take any chance of not getting our money out of us," Rhea said.

"These pictures were taken though, right?" Longarm prompted.

"Yes, of course. Taken by Wilson Maxwell. He'd come out from Vermont someplace. Set up a photographic studio on the corner of Block C. He was quite the artist, Wilson was."

"What happened to those pictures?" Longarm was starting to get impatient with these fellows by now. This could be his best possible lead, and neither of them seemed to appreciate the significance of their information.

"Burned up. Like I said already," Rhea said.

Longarm tried to put a rein on his impatience.

"There was a fire in the studio. The pictures burned up. At least I suppose they did."

"What about Wilson Maxwell? Even if the prints are burned, maybe the negative plates were saved. I could try and locate Maxwell even if he's left Oak Creek now. He might still have those plates," Longarm said.

Dyche shook his head. "Wilson died in the fire, Longarm. He's buried in our cemetery along with Tucker and Moffat and Reeb West. It was Reeb's murder that brought the Rangers here so that we found out the truth. Anyway, Wilson is buried there too."

"Damn," Longarm said. So much for that good idea.

Another point occurred to him, though, and he asked, "How did this fire happen?" Amos Vent was leaning close too now, his interest aroused right along with Longarm's.

Both Dyche and Rhea shrugged. "Who knows? Photographs use chemicals. We all know that. We've just assumed the fire started from the chemicals."

Longarm was no expert on photography, but as far as he knew the chemicals used in the photographic process stank and stained but weren't particularly flammable.

"When did the fire occur?" Vent asked, giving Longarm a sideways look that said they were both having the same train of thought.

"Pardon?"

"Was it before William Mann was exposed as a fraud? Or after?"

"Oh, dear," the mayor said, clearly shocked by the idea these law officers were raising. "I never thought to question..."

"After," Rhea said firmly. "It was just a couple days after Mann killed Tucker and Moffat and fled."

Longarm grunted. Another theory shot to hell.

He'd been thinking maybe Billy Two's impersonator murdered this Wilson Maxwell and destroyed the negative plates in an effort to avoid leaving any evidence of his real identity.

But if the fire and Maxwell's death occurred after the phony Mann ran out of Oak Creek . . .

"Damn shame," Amos Vent sympathized. "I thought you were onto something there. If it helps though, Longarm, maybe our people in Austin can dig up some old pictures of Billy Mann. They'd be daguerreotypes, not this modern process, but they'd be good enough for putting on a Wanted flyer."

"Thanks, Amos."

Longarm, of course, was interested in proving that the confidence artist who ran the Oak Creek scam was *not* Billy Two. But Amos Vent didn't know that. Amos was trying to be helpful. It wasn't his fault that old pictures of Ranger Mann were not at all what Longarm had in mind here.

Longarm sighed. "Look, gentlemen, we've been talking for hours, and personally my head is starting to swim around in circles. What say we break for lunch and talk some more after."

The mayor smiled and stood. "My pleasure, Longarm. And my treat. I insist."

Longarm shook hands with Mike Rhea, then leaned back and crossed his boots at the ankles. He reached for a cheroot while Amos was pulling out his tobacco plug.

"Son of a bitch covers his tracks pretty good, doesn't he," Longarm observed.

"He oughta know how," Amos agreed. "After bein' on the bright side o' the law so long."

Longarm ignored that opinion and tried to concentrate on all the many stories he'd heard through the day. There had to be *something* there that would help prove Billy Two's innocence.

Chapter 8

Longarm, Amos Vent, and Mayor Merle Dyche walked down the street toward the gutted remains of what once had been a photographic studio, an after-dinner cheroot clenched between Longarm's teeth while the other two gnawed on toothpicks instead.

"Right here," Dyche said, even though the assistance was far from necessary. There was only one empty, blackened foundation in sight. "This was Wilson Maxwell's place."

Longarm tapped the ash off his smoke before it got long enough to fall of its own accord and dribble down the front of his vest. He walked over to the ruins and stepped into the heap of charred timbers and twisted trash that the fire had left behind.

The destruction was a week or so old according to what the mayor had said, but there was still a heavy stink of lingering smoke lying over the junk heap that so recently had been a man's dreams and future hopes.

Longarm noticed too that the site had already been pretty

well picked over by others. He could see impressions in the soil at the corners that showed where carefully shaped foundation stones had been emplaced by Wilson Maxwell. The stones were missing now. Someone else had already appropriated them for re-use.

The same or other trash pickers had also sifted through the mess reclaiming nails, hinges . . . whatever might have been useful in the aftermath of the blaze.

A few of the sturdiest timbers survived with corrugated charcoal surfaces, but there was little on the blackened lot by now that could be of use to anyone.

The back end of the site must have been Maxwell's living quarters. The remains of a steel bed frame lay in the rubble there along with the usual oddments of everyday life, like a broken thunder mug, a wash basin bent out of true by the intense heat, a heap of half-burned clothing, a boot sole with the uppers missing.

Nearer to the street where the studio would have been, Longarm could see a twisted steel frame that might once have been the body of a large-view camera, but the fire had consumed the wooden sides of the camera box and the leather bellows. The remains of a ground-glass lens were cracked and discolored, and the beveled brass fittings were warped.

In the litter he could identify trays and broken beakers that must have been used in the chemical developing processes, and assorted bits of hardware that once had been attached to cunningly constructed items that only another photographic artist would recognize now.

A glass stirring rod that seemed untouched by the devastation of the fire lay half buried in a mound of ash. Longarm bent, picked it up and wiped it clean. It was damned little to be left now to show for a man's lifetime of toil. He tucked the glass rod absently into a pocket.

"How did Maxwell die?" he asked Dyche.

"Got it when the chemicals went up is what we assume," the mayor said. "We found him over there, just to the right of where you're standing. Near those tray things you see there. So we figure he must have been working at something even though it was late at night when the place went up. Must have forgotten to do something or got up and decided to do something in his studio when he couldn't sleep, something on that order. Whatever the reason, he was in here, in what he called his laboratory, when the fire started. At least this is where we found him when things cooled down the next day. Not that there was so much to find, you understand. What little was left of him wasn't hardly recognizable as having been a human person. He was burnt up awful bad."

"Late at night, you said? And he was working in the studio?"

Longarm's brow wrinkled in concentration. He knew damn little about the photographic process, but what smattering of information he did have led him to believe that the development of negative plates into photographic prints required strong, direct sunlight. Lamps and lanterns just didn't give a light that was bright enough or even enough to allow a good result.

Or so he believed. He could be wrong about that, particularly with the way science kept improving on things almost as fast as the new processes came along.

"That's right," Dyche said. "Two, three o'clock in the morning it would have been. Somebody saw flame coming out the windows and rang the fire bell. Roused everybody out, but of course there wasn't much we could do about it. We don't have a fire company yet, though we're talking about organizing one. We got people organized into a bucket line between here and the nearest well, but the best we could hope for by then was to keep the fire from spreading. We didn't even try to save the studio. Mind, at the same time we didn't know Wilson was still inside. We concentrated on wetting down the roofs and walls of Harry's place over there and Corliss's store over on that side. I got to tell you that even if we'd known Wilson was inside, by that time there wasn't anything we could've done to save him. The place was solid fire inside, and there wasn't any screaming like you'd expect if somebody was trapped alive inside it. We just didn't know, you see.'' Dyche still sounded upset that they had failed to try to reach Maxwell even though the man surely must have been beyond help by the time an alarm was raised.

Longarm clucked sympathetically and high-stepped his way through the litter back to the street. "I'm sure there wasn't nothing you could've done by then," he said.

"Lordy, I keep telling myself that." Dyche shuddered. "Can't think of a much worse way to die than burning up and being conscious to know it was happening."

Amos Vent grimaced and turned his head to spit. Longarm didn't blame either one of them. Fire would be a lousy way to go under.

"I notice a file cabinet over there," Longarm said, changing the subject, "but it looks to be empty."

"What's your point, Longarm?"

"Well, if that's where Maxwell stored his negative plates, for instance, why aren't they there? I was hoping if we could find an undamaged negative of the photo Maxwell took at your ceremony, or even a part of the plate just big enough to show the face of William Mann, it might be a help."

"If the plates are missing, Longarm, I think I know who would have them now," the mayor said. "My brother Monroe's Alex is an artist and is interested in the photographic process. I think Alex picked through the junk some. Might've taken whatever negative plates were left too. Do you want me to ask?"

"Dang right I do."

"All right, no problem. I happen to know that Alex is out sketching some landscape scenes this afternoon. I won't be able to find out for you until dark or thereabouts. If you want to wait that long."

"I want to wait," Longarm assured him.

"You need me for anything, Longarm?" Amos asked.

"Not really."

"I'd better get back down t' Coldwater in case your man

from Fort Smith shows up," the Ranger said. "I'm supposed to meet him, after all."

"Ask Mrs. Cates to hold my room for me, Amos. I'll be down to collect the rest of my things when I get a chance."

"I'll see you in a day or two then," Vent told him.

"I'm assuming I can find a room here for the night," Longarm said to the mayor. Most of his things were still at the rooming house in Coldwater so he would prefer a bed to a campfire tonight.

"I have empty rooms at my place. You're welcome to your pick."

Longarm nodded. He and the mayor turned back toward Dyche's saloon, and Amos headed toward the horses to start his ride back into Texas. It was late enough in the day by now that it would be well after dark before the Ranger got back to Coldwater.

Chapter 9

Longarm sat in the tiny lobby area of Merle Dyche's hotel with his boots propped on an ottoman and a cheroot between his teeth. A few yards away the saloon, which at this time of day doubled as a restaurant, was doing a slow but steady trade. Longarm had a newspaper open in his lap. The paper was months old and had somehow found its way here from New Orleans. The news in it wasn't much for being new. But the paper was the only reading matter in sight, and reading it beat going into the saloon for a supper he didn't want quite yet after having lunch so late.

Monroe Dyche came in, saw Longarm and smiled. Monroe was a slightly thinner version of Merle and had a little more hair than his brother. Otherwise he looked enough like Merle that they might have been twins, although earlier Merle had said that he was two years older than Monroe.

Longarm smiled back and laid his paper aside. He got quickly to his feet.

He was smiling at much more than Monroe Dyche's presence. Accompanying the younger Dyche—Mrs. Monroe Dyche?—was a damned fine looking young woman.

Lucky Monroe if a man his age had found himself a wife so young and, from what little Longarm could see of her, pretty. Second wife, obviously, if Monroe had a son old enough to be an aspiring artist.

The girl—woman really, she was in her middle twenties or thereabouts—was tall and slim, with chestnut-colored hair and pale gray eyes. Longarm couldn't see much of her because she was wearing an ankle-length duster and a sunbonnet, so that her hair and eyes and general dimensions were all he could really get a good look at.

Monroe Dyche seemed proud to be seen with her. And no wonder. Longarm would've been too.

"Monroe. Ma'am."

"Evening, Marshal," Dyche greeted him. "Merle said you wanted to see us?"

"Actually it's your son I need to see," Longarm told them.

Monroe and the lady looked at each other with grins and then began to laugh.

"Pardon me?"

Monroe, still grinning, looked back at Longarm. "A little family joke, Marshal, that happens often. Usually deliberately, to tell you the truth. I hope you don't mind."

"Reckon I don't though I still don't know what you're talking about, Monroe."

Dyche chuckled again and winked at the lady at his side. When he turned back to Longarm he said, "I have no son, Marshal. Just Alexandra here." He pointed toward the young woman. "My tomboy daughter, Marshal. Alex."

Both of them seemed to be getting a kick out of the harmless and often repeated tug on a stranger's leg.

Longarm went along with it, chuckling and expressing an appropriate amount of amazement before he got to the point of the meeting.

"Your uncle tells me you're an artist and a budding photographer, Miss Dyche."

44

"Alex," she corrected. "Please call me Alex, Marshal Long." Her voice was surprisingly deep and throaty. It came out almost a harsh whisper.

"If you wish, Alex. My friends call me Longarm."

"Good. Alex and Longarm it shall be." She extended a small, gloved hand for him to touch in a polite handshake to seal the bargain.

Longarm smiled. "I was gonna invite you folks for a drink," he admitted. "But that was when your dad had a son, Alex. Now I'm not so sure what I oughta do."

That seemed to please Alex, and her father too. They looked at each other and laughed. Alex turned back to Longarm. "I've only now gotten home, and I haven't had time for supper yet. Could we talk in the restaurant while I have something to eat, Longarm?"

"That'd be fine."

The three of them entered the double-duty saloon. There were two other respectable women dining with their husbands in the place, and Alex seemed to feel no discomfort about being in her uncle's bar at this hour. Apparently this dual role for the room was accepted as ordinary here. The patrons who were there to drink were doing so with quiet circumspection while the ladies were present.

Alex led the way to a shadowy back corner of the place and selected a chair that put her back toward the bar. Longarm held the chair for her and took the seat opposite her with Monroe seated between them to Longarm's left.

"Would you like me to take your duster and bonnet, Alex?" Longarm offered.

She shook her head. "I'll keep them, thank you."

The way the bonnet shaded most of her face was mildly annoying. All he could see of her was the bright sparkle of her eyes, and with the duster buttoned to her throat and its collar turned up, he really could not see much of Monroe's daughter Alex.

"We aren't fancy around here, Longarm," Monroe said. "Merle doesn't have service off a menu. You take what he serves or pick up something light off the free-lunch spread."

"What Uncle Merle serves is generally stew," Alex added. "Believe me, you don't want to know what he puts into it." She laughed.

"I'm always game for mystery and adventure," Longarm said. "If you're willing to try it I reckon I am too."

Monroe held three fingers up, and the bartender nodded.

"Uncle Merle said you wanted to question me about the equipment left behind at Mr. Maxwell's studio?" Alex asked.

"That's right. He said you may have recovered some things."

"And so I did. Not that there was much left to recover."

"It's the negative plates I was hoping to locate." Longarm explained the need, not the full truth of why he wanted to find them but at least what he hoped to recover from the fire-blackened ruins. "It would be a big help in my investigation," he said.

He thought he could see a frown forming under the deep hood of Alex's bonnet. "I wish I could help you, Longarm. I truly do. Actually, Mr. Maxwell's negatives were what I most hoped to recover myself. He was quite an artist, and I had hoped to learn from his sense of composition, if I'd been able to save some of his work. But there wasn't a single negative that survived the fire, I'm afraid."

"That's a shame."

"And quite odd too," Alex said. "I would have expected some of the glass plates to survive. It isn't like glass is flammable. I'd hoped that if some of the plates survived I could clean the emulsions and make some prints from Mr. Maxwell's better negatives."

"I saw a steel file cabinet today. Is that where the plates were stored?"

"That's right. I was familiar with the studio, you see. Mr. Maxwell was teaching me about the photographic process, and I'd helped him in the studio many times. He kept his plates in padded metal containers. He was very meticulous with them. As of course a photographic artist must be with all his—or her—materials."

"Yet the plates didn't survive the fire," Longarm observed.

Alex glanced toward her father, then leaned a little closer to Longarm. "I'm probably reading more into this than it is worth, Longarm, but I wondered at the time if there was something funny about all those plates being shattered."

"Oh?"

"Did you notice today that the cabinet drawers were pulled open?"

He nodded.

"That's the way I found them, Longarm. All the drawers had been open at the time of the fire. At least I assume they must have been. I can't think of any reason for those drawers to have come open as a result of the fire. And every plate in the cabinet had been smashed. Not merely cracked, as heat might have done. They were all quite thoroughly shattered. Into tiny bits."

It was Longarm's turn to frown. Damned strange. Funny, Alex had said? Perhaps something more than funny, actually.

"Could anyone else have been into the file cabinet before you? Looking for money or valuables, perhaps?"

"Apart from the fact that no one in Oak Creek is the sort of person to destroy things wantonly, Longarm, I am quite certain that I was among the very first to look through Mr. Maxwell's things. I'm positive I was the first to start looking for things to save. We were all there on the street that morning, everyone in plain sight of everyone else. Mr. Maxwell's body had only just been discovered. I thought immediately of his lovely work and how it should be preserved. The steel of the cabinet was still quite warm to the touch when I tried to recover his negative plates. And those drawers were already standing open."

"We aren't selfish treasure hunters here, Longarm," Monroe put in. "And we are no vandals either. We found Wilson's cash box in the bedroom. Every penny of his money and everything else of real value was boxed up and sent back to his relatives in Vermont. There was an address book in the cash box with his money. We found his mother's address from that."

"Uncle Merle and Daddy made a special trip down to Coldwater so they could mail the package to Mrs. Maxwell," Alex said.

"There wasn't much. A hundred fourteen dollars and some items of jewelry. That sort of thing. No one here kept anything of value, I assure you, although we did try to recover what hardware and small items we could. The things we could put to use. I don't think that constitutes stealing, do you?"

"No, of course not," Longarm said quickly.

"And I certainly cannot imagine anyone in Oak Creek breaking things simply for the pleasure of wanton destruction."

"If anyone did destroy those plates, Longarm, it was a criminal thing to do," Alex added. "Simply criminal. Mr. Maxwell was a true artist."

Monroe patted his daughter's gloved hand. "No one would do a thing like that, dear. You know they wouldn't. The plates were destroyed in the fire. Don't become overwrought, dear. Please."

Longarm, though, thought the loss of the plates more than a little suspicious. Flat plates of glass protected inside a steel cabinet should have been roasted, perhaps cracked. But shattered? That seemed damned unlikely.

"Perhaps tomorrow," he suggested to Alex, "you could go with me and we could have another look inside that cabinet? I wouldn't know what I was seeing, but you might. Maybe we can find some fragments that would still be usable."

"If you like," Alex agreed.

The conversation was interrupted by the arrival of three bowls of a thick, aromatic stew. The meat in it, Longarm suspected, was prairie dog. He smiled to himself. Alex might not want to know what it was, but he certainly had no objection. The flavor of prairie dog is delicate and faintly sweet. Much better than rabbit, in fact, and no one objects to that.

Alex Dyche, oddly enough, kept her duster buttoned, her bonnet on and her gloves in place as she ate. A tomboy, her father had called her. Quirky too, Longarm added silently. But then everybody is entitled to a little harmless eccentricity if they please. He put it out of mind and concentrated on enjoying a thoroughly good prairie dog stew.

"I can meet you here first thing in the morning, Longarm," Alex suggested when they were done eating, and father and daughter prepared to return to their home, wherever that was.

"That'll be fine, thanks."

"Until morning, then." Alex offered her small hand for him to shake again and turned away.

Longarm remained in the saloon. By now the dinner patrons were leaving, and the place was reverting to the masculine refuge it was at other than mealtimes. He was wondering if he could find a touch of Maryland rye whiskey behind Merle Dyche's bar or if he would have to open his own traveling bottle for a nightcap.

Chapter 10

"Anything else for you, Marshal?" the barman asked as he cleared the empty stew bowls away.

"You wouldn't happen to stock any Maryland distilled rye, would you?"

"No, sir. We have something that's called rye, but I think it comes out of St. Louis. I wouldn't say that it's much good, to tell you the truth. Not from what the gentlemen tell me, anyway. We don't sell much of it."

"Is there anyplace else that might have some decent rye?"

The bartender smiled. "I wouldn't know one whiskey from another myself, Marshal. I don't drink. But there's another saloon that opened up recently. You might try down the street." He pointed. "All the way to the end of town on the left. You can't miss it."

"Thanks."

Longarm was in no great hurry. It wasn't particularly late, and he wasn't particularly sleepy. And he certainly hadn't anything better to do than start a quest for the best rye available in Oak Creek. The young community was notably shy when it came to nightlife. There weren't even any card games in progress in Merle Dyche's saloon.

He took his time about trimming the end off a cheroot, warming it and getting a good coal glowing. Finally he stood and ambled outside.

Oak Creek at night would have been a bust for a partying sort of man. The street was nearly empty, and the few lights showing all seemed to be coming from back rooms where the townspeople had their living quarters.

Dyche's hotel and saloon was the only place at this end of town that showed lamplight from its street-side windows. Off in the direction the bartender had indicated Longarm could see another dim spill of yellow light reaching the street. Maybe for a change someone had been accurate when they gave directions and then claimed the place couldn't be missed.

Longarm wandered down that way, enjoying the cool of the evening. The high-plains air smelled clean and fresh now that the dust of the day's activities was settling. Longarm yawned. He wasn't tired. Just lazily relaxed.

As he neared the corner where Wilson Maxwell's studio had stood there was a smoky, unpleasant intrusion on the freshness of the air. The ash and half-burned wood stank.

Longarm reached the corner and paused. There was no point in looking through the ruins again tonight. There would be time enough for that come daylight and Alex Dyche's assistance.

Still, he couldn't help wondering what might have happened here.

Wilson Maxwell was dead. More to the point, the photographer's negative plates were conveniently shattered.

Convenient, that is, from the viewpoint of the murderer who had been impersonating Billy Two in this town.

Longarm had to consider the possibility that the false William Mann had had the balls to sneak back into Oak Creek and destroy those plates. The photos would have been hard evidence that could be used against him in a court of law. He would have known that. He might have wanted them destroyed and felt strongly enough about it to undertake the job in the middle of the night.

That would explain why Wilson Maxwell would have been in his laboratory late at night. He might have heard the sounds of the intruder, heard the sounds of his precious negatives being broken. He might have come into the laboratory to investigate and surprised the murderer there.

Dyche had said Maxwell's body was badly burned in the fire. No one would have thought to look for evidence of foul play in his death. The natural assumption would be that the town photographer died in the fire.

Longarm grunted. There were some things he was going to have to remember to ask Alex Dyche come morning. She'd said Maxwell had been teaching her about the photographic process, after all. Maybe she could help.

Or then again, maybe Longarm really was reading more into this than was there to read.

There just wasn't any way to know at this point.

Longarm set off down the street again in the direction of the town's other saloon.

The ash that had been building on the tip of his cheroot crumbled at the soft jar of his footfall. It rained down onto his vest.

Longarm grumbled silently to himself and stopped so he could brush the gray residue away. There wouldn't be a dry cleaner in a town this size, and he hated having to walk around with stains on his clothing.

A pale, shadowy presence flitted half-seen in front of him. Something small and indistinct like a tiny bird flying through the night. Except this small thing made a soft, soughing noise as it passed through the air. Almost at the same moment Longarm heard a light, twanging thump to his left. And a moment later he heard the dull impact of something striking the earth and ricocheting away.

Oh, shit!

He dropped to his belly, the .44–40 Colt Thunderer in his hand before he hit the ground.

That had been the sound of an arrow swishing through the air in front of his belly.

And the soft thump of a bowstring that accompanied it.

Longarm scuttled forward on hands and knees to the shelter of a fallen timber in the remains of what had been Wilson Maxwell's studio.

He wasn't thinking about keeping his damned clothes clean right now.

He was thinking about the would-be killer out in front of him in the night somewhere.

Where . . . ?

He heard almost at the same moment the harsh thud of something striking the other side of the charred wooden beam he lay behind and the lighter, softer thump of the bowstring twanging.

And still he could see no target to shoot back at.

Nothing was visible in front of him except shadow.

He could see no form, no movement that was threatening.

Nothing.

A damned bow is nearly silent if not quite absolutely so. And worst of all it has no flash of fire or gout of smoke to give itself away. Unless he could see the bowman himself, Longarm had no way to tell where the arrows came from.

No, he corrected himself. He had *one* way.

He lifted himself to his knees and peered across the blackened timber. He was not looking into the shadows now, though. Instead he looked for the arrow that had embedded itself in the other side of the wooden beam.

There.

The feathered shaft was barely visible in the dark. Only the fact that the pale wood of the shaft stood out in contrast against the black of the ash and charcoal behind it allowed Longarm to spot it.

The notched and feathered end of the arrow pointed slightly toward the right, toward the back end of the building Merle Dyche had said belonged to someone named Harry.

Longarm dropped back below the line-of-sight protection

of the timber and shifted quietly to his right until he came to the end of the beam.

He knew where to look now, but still he could see no target toward which he could return the deadly, silent fire.

Almost as bad was the fact that ordinary cover gives damned little protection from a bowman.

A man hiding behind a log or a rock is relatively safe from a man with a rifle. A bullet travels in a fast, flat arc that drops only inches for the first hundred yards or more of its flight. Duck out of sight and a rifleman can't hit you.

But an arrow moves slowly in a rainbow arc. A man who knows what he is doing with a bow can loft an arrow over a protective obstacle and with a little luck find his target anyway.

If the guy out there in the darkness figured that out . . .

Longarm moved again. Fast.

He heard the faint twang of the bowstring. This time there was a noticeable delay before the arrow dropped in, striking almost vertically out of the night sky, burying itself inches deep into the hard earth, landing less than three feet from where Longarm lay.

This shit had to stop, Longarm decided. Before the bowman turned lucky.

Longarm moved again, came to his knees and ripped three quick shots from the Thunderer toward the back wall of Harry's building.

The roar of the big Colt shattered the quiet of the evening, and the muzzle flashes from it destroyed Longarm's night vision.

Hopefully it also startled the crap out of the bowman and messed with his night vision too.

Longarm threw himself behind the timber again and rolled quickly to the side.

He blinked, fighting to get his night vision back and knowing there wasn't a damn thing he could do to speed the process.

On the street behind him he could hear shouts now, and

lights began to appear in one street-side window after another.

A match flared behind a window on the back of Harry's place.

Longarm caught a fleeting glimpse of cloth. A trouser leg, perhaps.

Then he heard the pounding of footsteps as the man with the bow raced away into the shadows.

The light from Harry's back window intensified and steadied as the match was applied to a lamp wick, and a patch of yellow light spread over the ground where the silent ambusher had just been.

Longarm jumped to his feet and began to give chase to the bowman.

He knew even as he did so that the attempt was a vain one. The bowman had had time to get away.

Longarm tried to run the son of a bitch down anyway.

Chapter 11

"Jesus, Marshal. I can't believe it. An Indian attack. Right here in the middle of town." The man shook his head in wonder and stared at the three arrows that had been recovered and now lay on top of the crude bar in Oak Creek's newest saloon.

Longarm grunted noncommittally.

The truth was that he couldn't believe it either.

But then the reason Custis Long did not believe it was that it wasn't so.

There hadn't been any Indian attack.

It hadn't been any wandering Comanche or Kiowa or Kiowa-Apache who tried to cut Deputy Long down with these arrows.

It had been . . . He sighed. Shit, he didn't know *who* it had been.

But it hadn't been any kind of Indian raid. He was sure of that.

An Indian warrior *might* decide to show everybody how

brave he was by sneaking into a town and lifting an easy scalp or stealing a horse or two.

But no sane Indian was likely to stand in and make a fight of it once his presence was discovered under those circumstances.

No, this thing tonight had been a deliberate ambush attempt on the part of somebody who had more in mind than a little casual coup counting.

"What tribe was he, Marshal?" someone else asked.

If nothing else, the nocturnal shooting had brought the town awake and seemed to be doing much for the business of the saloon. Half the grown males of Oak Creek seemed to be on hand for the aftermath of the excitement, a good many of them wearing night shirts stuffed haphazardly into their trousers.

"Pardon?" Longarm asked.

"I said what tribe of Indian was it that made this here arrow?" The man picked up one of the offending articles and gave it a critical looking over like he'd never seen such a thing before in his life. For that matter, Longarm decided, maybe he hadn't. Most of these folks had come from the East real recent.

"Yeah, Marshal," another man put in. "We hear you can tell what tribe an Injun is from by his arrows."

"You heard I could tell such a thing?" Longarm asked.

"Well, I mean... not you in particular maybe... but that somebody as knows the plains can tell." The man's voice sounded almost accusing now at the thought that this rough-and-ready frontier marshal might not possess such information.

Longarm smiled. "Don't believe everything you hear, friend," he advised. "And you're apt to hear just damn near anything out here. Take most of it with a grain of salt."

He picked up another of the arrows off the bar and turned it over in his hand. "One arrow is pretty much the same as another. They're made with whatever wood is handy for a shaft and whatever material is available for a point and whatever feathers happen to be around. Iron points like this you can buy in any trading post from Canada clear down into Mexico. And you see there aren't any special markings or paint on it. The shaft is bare, scraped willow. Even if the shaft had been painted, as most but not all Indians do, it wouldn't tell me anything unless I happened to personally know the man or the clan or the warrior society that favored those particular markings. And it can be any of those that decide on a kind of marking and use it. But it isn't like one tribe all uses this marking and all of some other tribe favors some other paint scheme. A fella makes them however he likes. Maybe he'll make all his one way and then maybe tomorrow he'll decide he wants to do something different. Anybody who tells you he can look at an arrow and give you its maker's life history from it, he's having himself some fun with you because you don't know any better.

"Some things you can tell by. The way lodge poles are arranged or lodge skins cut, the way moccasins are sewed or baskets woven, some of those things are pretty distinctive. But a plain arrow with no medicine markings on it, that won't tell you a damn thing, friend."

The pilgrims looked disappointed. What the marshal was telling them wasn't at all what they had been led to believe.

"I also heard that Indians won't fight at night," another man injected.

"Count on that," Longarm said with a smile, "and your hair could end up decorating somebody's lance. An Indian will fight wherever and whenever he's got a fight to make. Same as you or me. But that isn't something you have to worry about much. There isn't a hostile bunch within two, three hundred miles of here that I know about. Not at the moment anyhow."

"But . . ." The man looked at the arrows on the bar.

"It wasn't no Indian shot at me tonight," Longarm said.

The men in the saloon didn't like hearing that. Most of them, he saw, did not believe it. Well, they were entitled to their opinions. They were welcome to believe what they wished.

Longarm suspected that the next mail leaving Oak Creek would include eastbound tales of swarming Indian attacks regardless of what Custis Long or anybody else might tell them.

And the men of Oak Creek were entitled to that exaggeration too.

What interested Longarm, though, wasn't the matter of who hadn't shot at him tonight. But who *had*.

A wanted felon who had come here and now was afraid he would be recognized?

There was always that possibility. A man known to be a federal lawman never knows when the fear of arrest will drive a fugitive into doing something stupid. And it isn't only Indians who can shoot a bow. Archery was a popular hobby in much of the world. Including in the East of the U.S. of A.

It could be something as simple as that.

Longarm decided he would have to do some closer looking at the faces around him and see if he couldn't place any of them in the context of a Wanted poster.

In the meantime... He picked up his glass and finished the shot of rye he'd been served. The whiskey was too good to pour into the cuspidor but too poor to justify a second helping.

"If you'll excuse me, gentlemen, I think it's time for me to turn in." He laid a coin on the bar to pay for his drink and moved toward the door.

"Aren't you forgetting something, Marshal?"

"What's that?"

"Your arrows, Marshal. Don't you want them?"

"No, they don't fit a Colt so good. I don't want the damn things."

There was a dive toward the arrows on the bar as men pushed and shoved and cursed each other in an effort to grab souvenirs of the vicious Indian raid most of them seemed to believe had taken place in their town tonight.

Longarm left the eastern gentlemen of Oak Creek to their

delusions and headed back toward the hotel and a night's sleep.

He was walking with considerable more caution now, though, than he'd thought necessary earlier. A man who would try for him once just might want to dance again.

Chapter 12

Alex Dyche was waiting in the lobby when Longarm walked out of the restaurant after breakfast. She stood quickly and clutched at the top of her handbag, although he couldn't see any reason why the girl should be nervous about anything. Unless maybe she'd heard that someone tried to jump him last night and was scared of being in his company.

Again today she was wearing a light duster buttoned high to her throat and had on gloves and a deeply hooded sunbonnet.

Longarm wondered briefly if the budding artist was allergic to the sun or something. Except if that was the problem she wouldn't have needed to be bundled up indoors or at night like she'd been last night when he first met her. Not that it was any of his concern how she wanted to dress anyhow. It made a man curious, that was all.

They exchanged greetings, and Longarm asked her outright if she minded being in his company on the streets. She'd heard about the supposed Indian attack but said she wasn't concerned about that again in broad daylight.

"Just so you aren't uncomfortable to be walking with me," he said.

"No," she said in a quick, nervous yip. She swallowed and took a deep breath. "I mean, not at all, sir. I feel quite safe with you."

Longarm smiled and led her outside and down the street to the remains of Wilson Maxwell's studio. He was commencing to feel like he was more familiar with these fire-gutted ruins than he had any desire to be.

"The negative plates were stored in here," Alex said, leading the way through the rubble to the file cabinet. "See?"

Inside the drawers there was nothing but broken glass now. Very *small* bits of broken glass, each scrap showing streaks of light and dark that once would have made up the photographic images. The way so many plates had been broken and mixed together like that it would have been impossible for the most masterful jigsaw puzzle enthusiast to reassemble the bits into their original shapes.

"It wasn't heat from any fire that did that," Longarm said. For the plates to have been broken this thoroughly someone must have taken a hammer to them or crushed them the way a pharmacist will crush his chemicals with a mortar and pestle.

"Absolutely not," Alex agreed. "It is such a . . . waste. His prints were so wonderfully good. I can't help but think what a shame it was that Mr. Maxwell hadn't gone over to the new celluloid film process. That film isn't brittle, you know. It couldn't have been broken like this." She sighed. "But then I suppose if the negatives had been on film they would have burned. They would have been lost regardless."

Longarm grunted noncommittally. Alex Dyche knew a hell of a lot more than he ever would about this subject. Thinking of which . . .

"There's some things I've been wondering about, Alex."

"Like what, Marshal?"

"Longarm," he corrected with a smile. He wasn't sure

under the shade of the bonnet brim, but he thought she blushed a little as she bobbed her head.

"Anyway," he said, "there's some things that've been puzzling me. Like what Mr. Maxwell was doing in his studio in the middle of the night. He couldn't have been making prints, could he? And are any of the chemicals explosive or particularly flammable?"

"Oh, dear. I hadn't really thought much about that," Alex said. "I mean, everyone *assumed*..." Her gloved hand went to her throat in astonishment. "But no, of course he couldn't have been making prints. To do that... Longarm"—there was a small hesitation as she remembered to call him by his nickname—"you place the negative image in contact with a sheet of paper and lock both into a frame. There are the printing frames over there. What's left of them." She pointed. There wasn't any glass anywhere near them to indicate they had held negative plates when they burned.

"Then you have to expose the paper, through the negative that is, to direct sunlight for several minutes. Just how long it takes depends on the density of the negative and the strength of the sun. Part of the difficulty in learning the photographic process is learning to judge such things. It isn't at all exact. You have to learn how to judge what the correct balance should be. But you definitely need the strongest sunlight possible."

"You couldn't do it with a lamp, say?"

"Oh, no. The light would be much too poor. The light has to be uniform. That is even more important than it being strong. As for the chemicals, Longarm, none of them is flammable. They can be dangerous in other ways. The acids, for instance. But they couldn't possibly blow up or catch on fire. I don't believe you could make any of them burn even if you deliberately tried. It certainly couldn't happen by accident."

Longarm grunted again. "So there isn't any logical reason for Maxwell to be working in the laboratory late at night."

"There are a good many things you can do that require

no light. Many, in fact, do not permit light. But I happen to know from Mr. Maxwell's teachings that he never put off developing his images. He used the old wet-plate process, like I said, because that was the most advanced method available when he learned his skills. He never used the newer dry-film methods. Wet plates have to be developed as soon as possible after exposure or the emulsion dries out and loses clarity. When he photographed landscape scenes he even took his tent and wagon with him so he could develop his plates on the spot. He never delayed the process as much as ten minutes, much less waiting until nightfall."

Longarm's interest quickened. "Wagon, you say?" There weren't any burned wagon remains around the studio.

"That's right. Most photographers, particularly those who use the wet-plate process, carry their equipment in specially fitted wagons so they can be mobile yet still have everything with them when it is needed."

Longarm smiled. "You wouldn't happen to know where Mr. Maxwell kept this wagon of his, would you?"

"Certainly," Alex said. Then comprehension brought a smile to her lips. Longarm was barely able to see it there under the hood of her bonnet. "There could be some plates stored in the wagon, couldn't there?" she said with the same joy a grizzled prospector might display when he leaped out of a creekbed with a shout of *Eureka*.

"That's kinda what I had in mind," Longarm agreed.

"This way." Alex fairly ran through the ash and trash inside the studio foundations and into the alley where the archer had hidden himself the night before. Longarm had to stretch his legs to keep up with her in her excitement. Although if the wagon hadn't been disturbed to this point there was no reason why it should be in danger in the next couple minutes or so.

"Here," she said, tugging on the sagging door of a crudely constructed shed. "It's in here."

"Wait!"

Something—a sixth sense, or simply some sound or hint of movement that reached him on a level that was much too subtle to be consciously known but was felt nonetheless—made Longarm stiffen and cry out to the girl as she pulled the shed door open.

He was too late.

A blur of motion sped out of the interior of the shed toward Alex.

A feathered arrow shaft appeared as if by sleight of hand on the front of her loose duster.

The girl cried out and fainted, dropping to her knees and then toppling over backward into the dirt of the alley.

Longarm sprang forward, his Colt in his fist.

Chapter 13

Longarm jumped over Alex's legs, revolver extended. He lunged inside the shed, banging his shoulder painfully on the swinging shed door.

There was a blur of motion toward the back of the shed. A shadowy form dropping down behind the tall, boxy wagon that was parked inside.

Longarm threw himself belly-down into the dirt so he could snap a shot at the bowman underneath the chassis of the photographer's wagon.

The roar of the Colt was loud inside the confinement of the small shed, and the harsh smell of burnt gunpowder filled his nostrils.

Longarm mentally cursed himself as he heard the slug strike some metal part of the running gear and ricochet to slap harmlessly into the board walls.

He shifted to the side and fired again, but in the poor light, his eyes still accustomed to the bright daylight outdoors, he was unsure of his target.

Whatever, damm it, he had the son of a bitch cornered

this time. Longarm was lying in front of the only door leading into the wagon shed.

He blinked, his sight adjusting rapidly to the interior of the place.

There were some old crates and kegs piled against the back wall. The bowman, he suspected, was behind them.

He heard a scraping sound as if something solid was being moved aside.

"You might as well give yourself up before I have to take you the hard way," Longarm said loudly.

The noise he'd heard was repeated. But no one conveniently raised into view with hands uplifted.

"All right. The hard way," he said.

He moved to his right so he would be clear of the wagon body, then stood.

No one shot at him. Far as he could tell, nothing moved behind those boxes.

He held the Colt at the ready and took a cautious step forward.

Behind him he could hear Alex groan. She was alive then. Thank goodness for that.

Right now, though, damm it, he had no time to see to her. The bowman in front of him couldn't be allowed to escape a second time.

Longarm edged forward, ready to shoot at the slightest hint of movement from the back of the shed. Whoever the bowman was, there was no reason to think the man couldn't have a gun on him too. A bow is silent but awkward in close quarters. Longarm had to be wary of guns as well as arrows here. He inched forward one slow step at a time with the big Thunderer extended.

There was . . . nothing.

No movement. No sound. Nothing.

Alex groaned again. The girl was in pain, but right now there wasn't anything he could do about that. He had to flush out this son of a bitch who'd twice tried and twice failed.

Longarm reached the boxes and leaned cautiously forward. Now he was the one in the position of having to expose himself to the other's fire.

He looked behind the boxes.

And saw nothing.

"Shit," he said loudly.

There at the back of the shed, beneath the back wall, there was a gap between the boards and the earth.

There was more than enough room for the man with the bow to have slipped out underneath the wall and made his escape unheard through the alley.

There was no sign of man, bow, or arrows left now.

Longarm's first impulse was to drop down and follow the ambusher into the alley. He couldn't have gone far in broad daylight.

But behind him Alex Dyche cried out in her pain.

The girl was lying there with an arrow in her.

She could bleed to death if someone didn't see to her soon.

Longarm cussed under his breath and shoved the Colt back into his holster.

He turned and ran back to the shed door and knelt beside Alex's slim body.

The shaft protruding from the front of her duster hadn't penetrated very deeply into her flesh, but there was an ugly scarlet stain spreading into the cloth around the base of the arrow shaft.

The girl's eyes were open. They were large and pale and trusting.

"You're going to be all right," he told her. "Try not to move. You're going to be just fine."

Longarm took out his knife and as gently as he could began to cut the cloth away from the arrow.

Chapter 14

Alex Dyche looked at him with a deep, helpless pain in her pretty eyes, then turned her head away, unable to face him anymore. A tear welled slowly into view and then rolled out of sight down her cheek.

Longarm touched her chin and turned her head so that she was looking at him again. He smiled at her. "It's all right, Alex. Honestly."

She nodded, but there was a tremor in her lower lip that told him she didn't really believe that.

The problem she was facing was *not* the arrow that was lodged in her flesh.

That wound was bad enough but not truly critical. The arrow fired quickly by the jumpy bowman had struck Alex just above the slope of her left breast. She must have been half turned away from the man when it hit her, either because she was looking back at Longarm or because she was trying to turn and flee. The sharp steel trade point had pierced her upper breast at an angle and penetrated far enough that the tip of it was exposed now high on the side of her chest.

Some four or five inches of wooden shaft and steel point lay embedded inside the fold of living flesh.

But that was not the source of Alex's real pain.

The flesh the arrow had lodged in, and nearly all the skin around it that Longarm had exposed to view when he cut her duster and blouse away, was pink and puckered and silk-shiny to the eye. The nipple of her newly damaged breast was a tiny, twisted kernel of hard flesh that had never fully developed. It was misshapen and childlike.

The girl's whole body, at least all of it that Longarm could see, was a mass of scar tissue. She had been the victim of a fire a very long time ago, Longarm guessed. That, he realized, was the reason for the throat-high dusters, the always present gloves, the deeply hooded bonnets. She was ashamed of her own body and did not want to draw the cruel stares and comments of public exposure.

"It's going to be all right," Longarm said again gently.

On an impulse he leaned down and kissed her lightly on the forehead. Her bonnet had fallen nearly off when she hit the ground. He could see her face now. She was a pretty girl where the old flames had failed to reach her. Her face was delicate and fine boned and thin. But there was more of the ugly scarring on the side of her neck and at her throat.

Alex began to cry harder. But he thought she seemed relieved, too.

"This is going to hurt, Alex. I won't tell you otherwise. But the wound isn't dangerous. It should heal quick and clean."

"That doesn't much matter," she whispered. "Does it?"

"Oh, I reckon it does. But we'll talk about that later." He smiled and stroked the side of her cheek—it was unblemished and very soft—before he bent over her to do something with that damned arrow.

Behind him he could hear a rush of footsteps as townspeople were finally drawn toward the source of the gunshots.

Longarm straightened and turned. He motioned the men to stay back where they were. There wasn't any need for more help here, and he did not want Alex to be embarrassed by having more strangers than were absolutely necessary staring at her body.

"Stay right there, please, gentlemen," Longarm said firmly. "The lady is going to be fine but she don't need any commotion right now. I'll want a sheet or light blanket to cover her with in a minute here and some bandage pads and wrappings. You and you, go fetch me some, please. And you can get me a bottle of whiskey to sterilize this with. The rest of you turn around and hold folks back. We don't need any crowds." He turned back to Alex, giving no one room to argue with his judgment.

"Like I said, Alex, this is gonna hurt you some."

He took hold of the wooden arrow shaft—the arrow was a mate to those that had been fired at him the night before, plain and efficient and unremarkable—and pushed it deeper into her body.

Alex stiffened and bit at her underlip but did not cry out aloud. But then, he suspected, she knew how to deal with pain more than most folks would ever have to. The girl had had plenty of experience at hurting when she was burned in that fire long ago.

The arrow was hard to push through. Living flesh clamps down hard on anything that intrudes into it. Longarm had to apply considerable strength to make the rest of the sharp point push through the barrier of the skin that was containing it and pop out into full view.

"There," he said. "That's the hardest part."

Alex nodded and kept her teeth clenched.

Longarm used his knife to cut the point off the arrow. It took a full minute or more to get the job done because he had to whittle at the wood carefully, lest he jerk the shaft around inside her and cause even more pain than was necessary.

Finally the point separated and dropped to the ground.

"You doing all right, Alex?"

"Yes, thank you."

He smiled and winked at her and got a tiny, tentative

smile in return. This was one tough girl, he decided. She could damn well take it.

"Now another hard part."

Very carefully he trimmed and scraped the tip of the now bare shaft. He didn't want to leave any splinters in place that would act like barbs and hook into her flesh as he pulled the shaft free.

"Brace yourself," he warned.

Alex clamped her teeth tightly together and nodded.

A hard, clean pull and the arrow shaft slid free.

Alex grunted but didn't cry out. Most men Longarm knew would've screamed bloody murder, but she hardly made a sound.

Blood flowed freely once the shaft was removed, and Longarm let the wound bleed. He wanted the blood to carry off any dirt or specks of lint that had been carried into the wound by the arrow.

"You got those bandages and whiskey for me?" he called over his shoulder.

"Yes, sir."

"One of you bring them here. Keep your head turned, though. The lady don't need to be stared at."

"Yes, sir."

He heard the halting approach, turned and accepted the bundle that was handed to him.

Alex winced when he poured whiskey onto both ends of the long, clean wound. The caramel-colored whiskey diluted the bright red of the blood and made the girl's upper body a wet, pink mess.

"It looks good," Longarm said. He let the blood flow a few moments more, then wiped the wounds clean and applied a spill of whiskey one more time before he pressed wads of cotton bandage in place. He slipped an arm under Alex's shoulders so he could raise her off the ground enough to wind a wrapping around her and hold the pads in place to staunch the blood flow.

"You're doing fine." He could feel her tremble and shiver. "Is it still hurting that bad?"

"It isn't . . . that," she admitted.

Their faces were only inches apart. Her eyes were huge. And frightened. Longarm lifted an eyebrow.

Alex blushed. But she didn't look away. "I've never been this close to a man before," she whispered. "Not ever in my whole life. Except Daddy when he hugs me. And you're . . . so handsome." She said the last like it was an admission of a deep and horrible sin, and this time she did look away.

Longarm placed a fingertip against her jaw and again drew her face around toward him. "Is there anybody looking at us?" he whispered.

Alex's eyes shifted past his shoulder. "No."

He smiled. "Good."

Very lightly and tenderly he kissed her on the lips.

Alex gasped, and for a moment he thought she was fixing to faint.

"Let's get you back home," he said.

He took up the lightweight blanket that had been brought to him and covered her with it before he scooped her into his arms and stood.

Alex was smiling as the tall, lean deputy carried her down the main street of Oak Creek with a crowd of curious bystanders milling close around them now.

Chapter 15

Longarm hurried back to the wagon shed as soon as he had Alex comfortably settled into a bed in the living quarters behind her father's store. And as soon as he had a distraught and frightened Monroe Dyche calmed down as well.

Monroe was a widower, it turned out, who had raised Alex alone since her mother died in the same fire that scarred Alex when she was only eight. The man crumbled when he discovered that his only child had been shot. In many ways he seemed worse off than Alex did after the assassination attempt. Longarm had no time to comfort him now, though. The man with the silent bow and the nasty habits was still in town somewhere. And Longarm wanted him. He promised Monroe that he would come back later to check on Alex's wound. There was no doctor in Oak Creek, and the town barber had no formal barber-surgeon training. That seemed a damn shame. Longarm knew a good many barbers who were better doctors than certified physicians, at least when it came to common wounds. The way he'd heard it, barber schools had taken to the practice of cleanliness even before the medical universities had, and a good barber could save many a life as well as cutting a head of hair. If Alex was to be seen to, though, it looked like Longarm would have to apply his own experience. The eastern men who populated Oak Creek seemed to've had little experience with gunshot wounds and none at all with arrows. Longarm wished he could say the same but definitely couldn't.

Merle Dyche went with him when he went back to the wagon shed where the bowman had been hiding. There had been a reason, after all, why Longarm and Alex had gone there to begin with. The assault hadn't changed that, only delayed it.

"Are there any strangers in town that you know about, Merle?" Longarm asked as they walked.

The pudgy mayor shrugged. "We're still a new and growing town, Marshal. You could say that the whole place is full of strangers. Folks come in most every day from one place or another, still answering those ads Mann and his cronies placed. They come in and learn the truth and three quarters of them turn right around and go elsewhere. The other quarter, though, is like me and Monroe. They've already paid their money; they figure they're entitled to a plot of ground and the new start that was promised to them. They unload whatever they've brought and say they'll stick it out. So in answer to your question, hell yes the place is full of strangers."

Longarm frowned and tugged at his mustache. So much for the easy way.

Besides, he realized, it didn't necessarily hold that these attempts on his life had anything to do with Billy Two or the mission Billy One had sent him out on.

Some poor son of a bitch from Maine or New Hampshire or wherever could be wanted back home and be scared Longarm was going to discover him. Could be compounding his own problems now by trying to save himself by killing the federal officer before he was spotted.

"You know, of course," Longarm said, "that some bureaucrat could take a notion any time that you folks have to pack up and clear out. This is unassigned federal land. It ain't actually been opened to settlement, not under the Homestead Act or any other."

"We know that," Dyche said. "We also know that this is where we've chosen to stay." There was a stubborn determination in the man's voice that Longarm both understood and admired. But Longarm couldn't exactly tell Merle Dyche that.

"Just so you know. And I haven't been given any orders to move you out. You'd all best hope that I never do."

"We'd fight you, Marshal," Dyche said with a clear and simple sincerity. "Despite what you've done for my niece, Marshal, I would stand up against you too."

"Let's hope it don't come to that."

They reached the front of the wagon shed. Alex's blood still stained the ground beside the sagging door. Longarm motioned for Merle to stay back while he went in first. Just because the bowman had been flushed out once didn't mean the son of a bitch couldn't have come back for another verse of what had been basically a good idea. It might have worked just fine that first time if Alex hadn't been leading the way. Longarm palmed his Colt before he went in.

But the shed was empty this time, the air inside it baked from the sun's heat on the flimsy roof.

"Nobody home," Longarm said. "You can come in if you like."

The mayor joined him.

"I take it this was Maxwell's mobile studio?"

"That's right. He used it often."

The wagon looked like a military surplus ambulance that had been sheathed all around to create a boxy, light-proof structure. The body was painted a dark green, and the running gear and trim were black. The whole thing was utilitarian and plain. A door had been set into the back of the rig.

The inside of the thing was dark and smelled of chemicals. Longarm wrinkled his nose and felt for a lamp. He found a lantern suspended near the door and lighted it.

"Shit," he said aloud.

"Something wrong?" Dyche stayed outside but pushed his head in.

"Just what you'd expect." Longarm pointed. "He's been here before us."

The interior of the mobile studio was a shambles. Chemical containers had been broken. Drawers pulled out. Cabinets left open. The floor was littered with shards of broken glass that might once have been photographic negative plates.

Someone—the man with the bow? perhaps but not necessarily—had already been here. Whoever it was was taking no chances with Wilson Maxwell's negatives.

Longarm would be able to gather no evidence about the real identity of the fake William Mann in this quarter.

"Shit," he repeated.

"I'm sorry, Marshal," Dyche said. "I wish there was something we could do to help."

"You ain't the only one, Merle." Longarm extinguished the lantern and backed out of the shed, grateful for the fresher air once he was away from the stink of the chemicals. He reached for a cheroot and lighted it to help get the flavor of acid out of his mouth after breathing the chemical-tainted air inside the wagon.

The bowman might or might not have anything to do with William Mann and Longarm's assignment here. But this business with the studio and the wagon, that pretty much had to be related to Longarm's search.

*Some*body in Oak Creek didn't want Deputy Marshal Custis Long to uncover the truth about the men who had run this land scam in No-Man's-Land.

"Might as well go back to your place, Merle. I've got some heavy thinking to do."

Chapter 16

"Rye whiskey, Marshal? On the house."

"No, thanks, but I suppose a beer wouldn't hurt. I—" Longarm's train of thought was interrupted by a flurry of activity at the street entrance of the mayor's saloon. A man, the smith and harness maker who Longarm remembered meeting the day before, stuck his head inside and yelped, "Trouble coming, Merle. You better see to it." Then the man, Longarm thought his name was Pearl or Purl, something like that, spotted Longarm standing beside Merle Dyche; for some reason he blushed furiously and hurried back out onto the street.

Mid-morning drinks forgotten, both the mayor and Longarm followed him into the sunshine.

Amos Vent was riding in again, and again today he was accompanied by another rider. The newcomer wore a badge pinned to his vest too, and even from a distance it was plain that this man's badge was not the circle and star favored by the Texas Rangers. It was a federal shield worn on prominent display. Lew Campbell seemed to've arrived from Fort Smith.

Longarm smiled a little, thinking about Purl's discomfort. Yesterday they hadn't known it was a federal deputy riding with Amos. Today they did. And in Oak Creek, a federal officer meant trouble.

There wasn't much to smile about when it came to Lew Campbell, though.

The man wore his badge on his chest like it was a chip on his shoulder.

Longarm preferred to carry his tin out of sight and to adopt a loose and easy attitude toward the world, except when something different was clearly required.

Lew Campbell's posture and expression suggested it would be a positive pleasure for him if somebody, anybody, tried to fuck with him.

Perhaps, Longarm reflected as he leaned against the front wall of Dyche's building and reached for a cheroot, that was a reflection on the Fort Smith officer's small physical stature. Some little men did that. To compensate for lack of size they went heavy on outlook. Plumb mean, some of them were.

Deputy Marshal Campbell was about the size of an average twelve-year-old boy. But any resemblance to a kid stopped right there.

The man had muttonchop side whiskers and a ragged jungle of mustache. Whiskers, mustache and hair all could have used the attentions of a barber for a couple months past.

His hat seemed half again as big as he was, but even the shade of so huge a chapeau hadn't kept his face from weathering dark and leathery.

He had no coat on, perhaps because the tails of a coat might interfere with a quick draw, but the shirt under his black leather vest was crisp and starched, with a fresh collar attached and a gambler's string tie carefully positioned. His knee-high boots were freshly blacked and worn outside black broadcloth trousers.

Mostly, though, an observer would see his guns. A pair of them, one riding on his left hip and the other canted beside his belt buckle for a left-handed cross-draw. The deputy wasn't a showoff, Longarm realized, who pretended to be able to make smoke with both hands at once. He simply wanted more firepower available than comes in a single, six-holed cylinder and didn't mind who knew it. Likely he would have one or more hideout guns tucked away somewhere on him in addition to the pair of Colts he kept on display.

Longarm lighted his cheroot, flicked the spent match into the street and stepped down off the board sidewalk to greet Ranger Amos Vent and Longarm's colleague from Arkansas.

Amos smiled pleasantly as he made the introductions. Deputy Marshal Campbell's expression was what you might expect if he'd just stepped in something. When he accepted Longarm's offer of a handshake his grip was feather light and ended as quick as was decent. Or maybe a shade sooner. The palms of his hands were soft as a debutante's.

The man's hands, Longarm noticed, were unusual for so small a man. His fingers were exceptionally long. If Campbell had chosen to go into a different line of work he might have made a good cardsharp with hands like those.

"Pleasure to meet you," Longarm said. "Heard about you, of course. They say you get the job done."

Deputy Campbell made no such enthusiastic claims about Marshal Billy Vail's top deputy. He grunted and said, "This is my territory."

"So it is," Longarm agreed with a smile.

"The warrants for Mann are in my pocket."

"I'm sure they are."

"What are you doing here?"

"Don't you think we oughta discuss this someplace else, Deputy?" Longarm suggested. Aside from Amos Vent and Merle Dyche there were other townspeople of Oak Creek drifting closer now to hear what this second federal man had to say.

"No, I don't. Deputy." Campbell made the title sound almost like an accusation. Which seemed damned odd to Longarm, coming as it did from another guy who carried the same title and the same shaped badge.

Longarm shrugged. He didn't give a shit if Campbell didn't. "I think we're looking for the same fugitive. Deputy. I'm investigating some allegations made in New Mexico. I've heard, of course, why you are looking for him." Longarm never had exactly told Amos why he was looking for the fake Billy Two. The New Mexico invention should calm Campbell down, he figured, since the territory of New Mexico was within Billy Vail's jurisdiction.

For that matter, of course, any place in any state, territory or possession of the U.S. of A. was inside the jurisdiction of any federal peace officer. But Longarm got the notion that Deputy Campbell wouldn't be much impressed by that line of logical reasoning.

"You got warrants?"

"Nope. Like I say, I'm investigating here, not manhunting."

"Well, I got warrants."

"All right."

"Stay out of my case."

Longarm shrugged and drew on his cheroot. "I was assuming we could work together since we seem to be going in the same direction."

"We can't," Campbell said flatly.

That seemed to settle the question, in Deputy Campbell's mind, at least. He turned away as if dismissing Deputy Marshal Long from consideration and this time scowled at Merle Dyche.

"You people are illegally squatting on unassigned lands owned by the government of the United States of America," he said loudly enough for everyone within half a block to hear. "I order you to leave. Immediately."

Merle Dyche's jaw dropped. "But..."

"Immediately," Campbell repeated.

"But we..."

Campbell ignored the anxious, suddenly worried townsmen and turned to Amos, who at the moment was busy giving Dyche an apologetic grimace.

"Which way did Mann run when he left here?" Brisk, brusque, all business. Find the son of a bitch and shoot him. The quicker the better.

"Oh, now lemme see if I c'n recollect," the friendly Ranger drawled. He fingered his chin and screwed up his lips in a show of deep thought. Yesterday afternoon Ranger Vent had pointed out to Longarm the route the phony Billy Two's tracks had taken out of Oak Creek. Hadn't had to hesitate about doing it either. Apparently the Ranger didn't care for Deputy Campbell any more than the boys in Oak Creek did. Or, for the rest of that truth, much better than Custis Long did.

"C'mon," he said finally. "I'll show you." Amos swung back onto his saddle and backed his horse out of the still growing crowd.

Campbell followed him, but instead of politely backing away from the men he walked his horse through them. Considerate sort of fella, Longarm thought darkly.

"Don't any of you still be here when I come back," Campbell warned over his shoulder without even looking back to observe the effect of his orders on these hopeful, would-be pioneers from the East.

At least he waited until he was clear of the crowd before he put the spurs to his horse and cantered off after Amos.

"Whew!" someone whispered.

Longarm looked at the man and grinned. "Ain't that the truth."

Chapter 17

Longarm watched Amos Vent and Lew Campbell ride out of sight around the side of a distant building, then flipped the butt of his cheroot into the street and slipped quietly out of the crowd of Oak Creek townspeople.

These good folks would have some serious talking to do about now, and he figured they didn't need the presence of another U.S. deputy to hamper their conversations while they were doing it.

Besides, regardless of his personal opinions about Deputy Campbell, the man was acting right off the pages of the proverbial book.

And if he wanted to do that in such a way that he came across to the rest of the world like a horse's south end, well, he was entitled.

The point was, no matter what Custis Long's personal opinion might be—and he did happen to have one—his professional judgment said that he'd best keep his mouth firmly shut on this one.

That little slip Dyche had made yesterday showed that

Amos had been trying to give some helpful advice to these folks about how to maybe hang on to their truly illegal squatting claims.

Deputy Marshal Custis Long couldn't do any such thing.

There wasn't any way he was going to put himself in the position of advising somebody how they ought to go about breaking the same set of laws that he was sworn to uphold. A finagle or a wink was one thing. Busting holes in the law was another. Longarm could only go so far, and this deal in Oak Creek had the capacity to drag him into deeper water than he wanted to swim out of if these boys turned stubborn.

So he was better off, and the men here were better off too, if Custis Long made himself politely scarce while they were having their discussion behind Lew Campbell's back.

Merle was taking the crowd inside his saloon, so having a drink was out of the question for the time being. The town's other saloon would be closing down so everybody there could join the rest at the meeting now in progress.

Longarm settled for walking across the street and helping himself to a seat on an upturned keg at the front of Monroe Dyche's store.

It occurred to him that with virtually every man in Oak Creek assembling across the way, he had been presented an opportunity to give every one of them a looking over as they filed inside the mayor's saloon.

What he was hoping for, of course, was some clue as to which one of them might be the ambusher with the quiet bow and arrows.

The archer almost had to be one of the Oak Creek residents.

Longarm had already gotten a good look at the men who were on hand when Campbell issued his demand that the town be abandoned.

Now, as a succession of small boys ran to spread the word about the excitement, more and more people streamed in. More, in fact, than Longarm would have thought lived in the small, rawly new little burg.

He sat on the keg and smoked another cheroot and examined each face as the men hurried to the impromptu town meeting. And paid attention as well to each man's posture and gestures as they came close enough for him to see them. Was any of them trying to keep his face shielded, trying to remain half turned away, slouching or trying to seem inconspicuous.

He grunted unhappily as the stream turned to a trickle and then stopped altogether.

Not one face looked like any he remembered from the Wanted posters a deputy has to examine and stay up on week in and week out. But then, dammit, a deputy in Colorado doesn't pay all that much mind to posters coming out of New York or Massachusetts or the other places that these folks came from.

Anyhow nobody he saw set off any mental alarms that this one might be a fugitive from thus-and-such or that one could be on the run from this-and-that.

And none of them was considerate enough to walk down the street with a bow and a quiver of arrows in his hand.

Pity.

Longarm stood, his tendons creaking, and bit back a yawn. He flicked the stub of the cheroot into the street and wondered what he ought to do with himself to keep out of the way of the men of Oak Creek.

He could hear frightened and sometimes angry voices coming out of the door and the windows of the saloon.

Behind him there was a "Closed" notice set in the window of Monroe Dyche's store, although the door was standing wide open from where Monroe had rushed across the street to his brother's place with everybody else.

Longarm figured he might as well stop in and see how Alex was doing after her ordeal earlier this morning.

He turned and walked into the cool, shadowy interior of the mercantile.

"You aren't disturbing me. I wasn't asleep," Alex assured him. "I was just resting my eyes."

He pulled a chair closer to the side of her bed and sat

next to her. She lay under a down comforter, surrounded by plump pillows and the scent of clean sheets. The comforter was pulled high under her chin. The burn scars were not visible other than a tiny patch on the side of her neck where the comforter failed to cover her. She looked awfully pretty except for a bright, watery redness in her eyes.

"Resting your eyes?" he asked. "Looks more like you've been poking sharp sticks into them. Does it hurt that bad?"

Alex turned her head away and began to cry again.

"Do you want me to see if I can find you some paregoric or laudanum, something like that?"

"It isn't ... it doesn't hurt. Hardly at all. Honestly. Just a little dull aching, like."

"What is it then, Alex? Is it anything I can help with?"

She didn't answer. He could see from the trembling in her shoulders that she was still crying.

He got up and went around to the other side of the bed and knelt there so that he was face to face with her.

Alex squeezed her eyes shut tight and refused to look at him.

"Tell me. I'd like to help make it better if I can," he said gently.

"Sure." Her voice was suddenly bitter. "Make it better, Longarm. Rub an ointment on and make these scars go away. You've seen me." Her eyes snapped open, and she gave him an accusing stare. "You know what I look like, damn you. Can you make *that* better? Can you make it so that I won't sicken any man who ever looks at me? Can you even *pretend* that I'm not hideous and ... and ... and just *awful*?"

"Is that what this's all about?" He smiled and propped his elbows on the edge of her bed, leaning down closer to her as he did so.

"That," she agreed, "is what this is all about," and began crying again. "No gentleman would ever be interested in anything so ugly and deformed, Longarm. Nobody ever has. Nobody ever will. Never."

" 'Nobody' covers an awful lot of folks," he reminded

86

her, "and 'never' seems quite a while. Are you *sure* about this?"

"Positive," she said.

"Now ain't that interesting," he observed. "Course it just goes to show how much I still got to learn about folks. Because I never would've guessed it my own self."

"I know you are trying to be polite, Longarm. You needn't bother. I know what the truth is. Haven't I been living with it all these years? You couldn't know about that. But I certainly do. I've had to every day since it happened."

"Yes, I can see how your experience beats mine on the subject. Reckon I stand corrected, thanks. You mind if we change the subject?"

"Please do," she said. She poked a small, red-scarred fist out from under the covers and knuckled her eyes.

Longarm pulled out his bandanna, folded it carefully to make sure there was a clean spot showing, and used the wad of cloth to dab the tears out of her eyes for her.

"Thank you," she said.

"Any time." He smiled at her and gave her a wink, drawing a tentative smile in return. "So tell me," he said, "if you could make wishes come true, Alex, which would you rather be, pretty or beautiful?"

"Pardon me?"

"You heard me. Would you rather be a pretty woman? Or a beautiful one?"

She looked puzzled. "But they're the same thing. I mean, I suppose beautiful is prettier than just pretty. But they're really the same thing. And besides, I thought we were going to change the subject."

"We did. You were talking about scars and ugliness, I'm talking about the difference between pretty and beautiful. And they aren't at *all* the same thing, you know."

"They are too," she insisted.

"Not even hardly related," Longarm said with a grin. "Pretty . . . now personally I happen to think that you're pretty, but I know you wouldn't believe me about that so we won't try and get into it right now . . . anyhow, as I was saying before you rudely interrupted me, ma'am, pretty has to do with the way a person *looks*. Beauty, that has to do with the way a person *is*."

"I don't understand," Alex admitted.

"Think about it," Longarm told her. "Pretty is something that's on the outside. But beautiful, that's something that starts on the inside and kinda glows and shines its way through to the surface. Whatever the surface happens to look like." He grinned again. "And what I suspect about you, Alex Dyche, is that you're pretty *and* beautiful both at the same time. Which sure Lord ain't always so. A lot of awful pretty girls are far from being beautiful inside where it really counts. And a lot of beautiful women are nothing much to look at."

"You're trying to make me feel..."

"What I am trying," he said with a quiet sincerity, "is to tell you a very large, very simple truth about people."

"You saw my body. You saw how horrible I am. How ugly."

"I saw your body," he agreed. "I saw your pain. I saw how you dealt with that pain. I saw that you have nerve and strength and decency. As for your body, what of it? Your skin was burnt but not your mind and not your heart. You're still a beautiful girl, Alex Dyche."

She thought about that for a moment. Then relaxed. She even smiled. "Thank you, Longarm. Thank you for trying. You almost make me believe that someday I will find some man who isn't repulsed by what he sees when he sees me. It's just that so far I haven't been lucky enough to find a blind man."

Longarm laughed and said, "Okay, have it your way. I won't argue with you about it. While I'm here I expect I should look at that wound. See that it hasn't started to fester."

"This quick?"

"You never know. Don't want to take any chances, do we?"

"I suppose not." She pushed the comforter down to her waist, exposing herself to him for the second time that day.

When Longarm and Monroe had put the girl to bed they had slipped a light gown over her shoulders, but that was all she was wearing. Longarm unfastened the ties that held it together and pulled the flimsy cloth aside.

The makeshift bandage he had applied earlier was gone now, in its place a much smaller and tidier gauze pad that was plastered all around to hold it there. He tugged on the sticky plaster and exposed the softly rounded side of Alex's breast.

As he had expected, and as Alex herself had said only a moment before, it was much too early for any infection to be visible. The only red he saw was the red of the burn scar tissue that puckered her skin and made it unnaturally shiny.

The entry and exit wounds where the arrow had pierced her were small and dark with crusted blood.

"Does it look all right?" she asked.

"Just fine," he assured her.

He bent closer and ran a fingertip very lightly over the shriveled wisp of flesh that was her undeveloped nipple. Alex gasped. "Don't . . ."

"You felt that just fine," Longarm observed.

"Of course I did," she retorted. "Just because it was burned doesn't mean . . ."

He grinned. "Uh-huh. Just because it looks different don't mean it *is* different."

"That wasn't very nice of you," she said.

"Miss Alex, I am worse than simply not nice. Sometimes I am positively wicked." He grinned at her again and dropped his face to her.

Very lightly he kissed the twisted bit of nipple, then ran the tip of his tongue over it.

Alex's breath caught in her throat. "Please," she cried. Longarm honestly did not know if she was asking please yes or please no. He doubted that Alex knew either.

He touched her chest, deliberately pressing his hand down on top of her scars. Then he pushed the front of her wrapper aside to expose her other breast. The horrid scars ran across her body and down onto her side somewhere, but most of her right breast had escaped the damage of the fire. That nipple was full sized and firm, and the pink of it was a most healthy shade.

Longarm kissed that nipple too and sucked on it gently.

"Please," she whispered again. This time he was pretty sure it was a yes she was asking please for.

He smiled and shifted up a few inches so that his mouth was poised only fractions of an inch over hers. "If you really want me to stop, Alex, I will."

She squeezed her eyes shut. And shook her head vigorously from one side to the other.

He bent to her. Kissed her. Felt the quickening of her breath and tasted the sweet flavor of her mouth.

After only a moment Alex sobbed, the sound of it a mingling of anguish and joy.

Her arms came up to encircle his neck and she pulled him to her with a fierce, sudden strength, and now she was kissing him back.

Alex Dyche wasn't ever again going to be able to claim that no man could want or appreciate her or her scarred but still entirely alive and vital body.

Chapter 18

"You don't have to do this, you know."

"Yes, I do know." He pulled away from her a few inches and smiled, then bent to kiss her again.

Alex sobbed and held him tight, unmindful of her wound, not seeming to care about anything now except the feelings that were shooting and slashing through her slim, battered body. But this time the feelings were of an intense, joyous pleasure instead of the pain that had always been her norm.

She kicked the comforter out of the way and spread the light, kimono-like wrapper wide open so that her whole body was open to him.

A small, barely noticeable catch in her breath told Longarm that the girl still believed, in spite of all the evidence he had already given her, that he would see the scars on her body and at the last moment would turn away from her in rejection.

That, he figured, was one of the easiest fears in the world to dispel.

He sat upright on the bed at her side and deliberately looked her up and down.

If it hadn't been for the scars left by that long-ago fire, Alex's body would have been perfection itself.

She was slender but beautifully proportioned, her waist and wrists and ankles tiny, her breasts and hips swelling softly into sleek, inviting curves.

The ugly red scar tissue ran and sagged and flowed in a rough-formed pattern that trended diagonally from her left shoulder, down across her left breast where the bandage and plaster stood out starkly white against the shiny red of her flesh, then down across her flat stomach to end somewhere in the vicinity of her waist on her right side.

More free-form patches of scar marred the softness of her lower belly, intruding slightly into the glossy chestnut patch of curly pubic hair at her vee.

Her left thigh was blemished, and both her forearms and hands were a mass of scars from where she must have tried to ward off the burning cloth or wood or whatever it was that had contained her within the flames.

Longarm slowly and very deliberately looked her over from scalp to foot soles.

He even turned her over onto her stomach so he could see her back.

Unlike so much of the front of her body, the back of her was nearly unmarked.

A small patch of red was visible on the right side of her waist, another at the base of her neck.

Except for those, the skin he could see there was soft and creamy, practically glowing with health and vibrant energy.

Her back was exquisite. Soft shoulders and a prominent backbone, tapering to that impossibly tiny waist, then flaring again into a pert, rounded little ass.

Longarm grinned and bent to kiss first one tender cheek and then the other.

Alex squirmed and wriggled under his light touch.

"I can't . . . I can't believe . . . I never dreamed a man as handsome as you would ever want to . . . you know." She rolled abruptly onto her back again, facing him. Her eyes were filled with tears again, but this time he could see that they were tears of happiness. She was smiling up at him with trust and pleasure and perhaps something more, something on the order of infatuation. No more than that, he hoped. Shy, frightened Alex didn't yet know how to deal with infatuation, much less with love.

"I dreamed about you last night," she said softly. "Except not a real dream. I was awake. Imagining more than dreaming. I kind of . . . thought about how it would be . . . if you touched me."

"Like this?"

She smiled again. "If you kissed me."

"Like this."

"And if you . . ."

"Mmm. Like this."

He lay beside her, moved back and forth, shifted and curled and stretched. Touching her. Running his tongue over her. Suckling her nipples and mouthing her flesh.

Alex moaned and writhed as she discovered the sensations her body was capable of feeling. The damage to her was all on the outside. Within that scarred exterior she was a beautiful and desirable and responsive young woman.

"You, uh, aren't a virgin are you?" he asked.

"Yes. Do you mind?"

He hesitated. "I'll stop if you want, Alex. I don't want to. But I will if you say."

"No. Please don't stop. Please, Longarm."

"Then I reckon I don't mind. And I'll try and not hurt you."

"Hurt me? Just you being here with me, you being willing to kiss and hold and love me, that gives me more pleasure than any amount of pain could ever take away. I'm just sorry I don't know enough to be good for you, Longarm."

He smiled. "Not knowing things, Alex, that's something that's easily taken care of. If you want to learn, that is."

"I want to learn," she whispered. "For you."

"And for you too, I hope. For the both of us to savor and enjoy and take pleasure in."

"Yes."

He smiled and kissed her again, and this time Alex's hand crept between their bodies to find and hold and fondle him while they kissed.

"It's so big," she whispered. "Do you think it will all fit?" The question was asked in all sincerity, but Longarm couldn't help chuckling.

"It'll fit," he said. "That's a promise."

"Here?" She guided his hand to show where she meant rather than say the forbidden word aloud.

"There. Other places too if you like."

"Really?" She didn't sound shocked, just vastly interested. And perhaps excited as well by this discovery of an aspect of sex she'd never been told about before.

"Here," he said. "And here."

Alex's eyes went wide. "Really?"

"Uh-huh."

"You'll show me? Everything?"

"Everything," he promised.

"Starting?"

"Now."

"Good," she said firmly. "I want to know everything there is to know about how I can please you, dear." She stopped, her eyes going wide.

"Something wrong?"

The girl smiled. "Oh no, dear. Nothing could possibly be wrong now. And there. I've done it again."

He raised an eyebrow.

"I called you 'dear.'"

"So?"

"I've . . . never said that to a man before. Not to any man. I've never been kissed or touched or . . . anything. And I find that I like it very much. Kiss me again, please."

He obliged.

"And touch me again?"

"With pleasure."

"That feels soooo nice." She giggled. "Dear."

"Is nice too, by damn."

He nuzzled against her chest and lipped first the twisted, fire-ruined nipple on her left breast, then the healthy and turgid right nipple. Alex quivered and moaned.

He slipped his hand between her thighs. She was as wet there as if she'd just stepped from a bath, her body fluids warm and slippery to ease his entry.

First a light touch, then a scant inch or two of penetration. She gasped, but when she moved it was to lift her hips to him. There was no attempt to draw away from his entry.

"You're sure?" he asked.

"Longarm, if you don't ... you know ... do it ... right now, why, I think I shall just scream, dear."

He grinned and raised himself over her willing, receptive body, poising between her knees and lowering himself to her.

The tight and tiny rosebud of her sex was small but ready. Alex arched her back off the mattress eagerly, and Longarm lowered himself very slowly, very gently into her, sliding inside her a scant fraction of an inch at a time, giving her time to adjust to his entry and to accommodate him.

"Oh, my." Alex's eyes went wide as the head of his rigid form reached the thin membrane of her virginity. "I can feel it, dear. I can feel you. Inside me. So lovely. I can actually feel your pulse bumping and moving inside me there."

He smiled.

"More. Please. You aren't hurting me. In a little more. Yes. Now ..." He could feel the tension in her as she strained upward against him, could feel the resistance of her hymen.

Then suddenly the wisp of membrane parted, and he slid another inch deeper inside her. Alex gasped. And smiled. She was impossibly tight and hot around him.

"I'm a woman now, dear," she whispered. "Thanks to you."

" Mmm." He lowered himself farther, more quickly now

but still careful to give her time to accept the intrusion of his body into hers.

Alex gasped again and clutched him with a sudden fierce strength, locking her arms and legs around him and pulling him all the rest of the way inside herself until he filled her small body and she cried out with happiness at his presence.

"Oh, God."

"Nope." He grinned. "Just me."

"I love the way you feel there, dear."

"So do I, Alex," he said solemnly.

"I want to learn. I want you to teach me. Everything."

"Time for school to start," he whispered as he nuzzled her ear.

And he began to pump gently in and out of her hot, sensitive flesh.

Chapter 19

Longarm damn near got himself embarrassed. Or horse-whipped.

He had just finished dressing and was sitting on the side of Alex's bed pulling his boots on when he heard her bedroom door open, and the girl's father came into the room without knocking.

"Longarm?" the man blurted.

Longarm straightened, palming a cheroot as he did so and surreptitiously dropping it onto the floor. "Hello, Monroe. Excuse me a second here. Dropped a dang smoke someplace." He bent and retrieved the cheroot, then shifted over onto the chair that was still at the bedside. "Your girl seems to be all right, Monroe. I think she'll heal clean."

"You, uh, were checking on her?"

"Checking on her. Talking a little. Didn't think you fellas would want me listening in on what you was talking about. Is it all right for me to ask how things stand? Or would you rather not. I don't mind if you want me to keep shut on the subject."

Monroe Dyche looked at Alex with the down comforter tucked high under her chin again—although he couldn't know, or at least Longarm sincerely hoped that he couldn't know, the cover was there because she had felt a bit chilled in the sweaty aftermath of their third round of vigorous lovemaking—and then at Longarm. He peered from one to the other of them for a moment, then smiled and shrugged. The deputy had, after all, been the one to tend to his daughter's wound earlier.

"I suppose it won't be any secret," Dyche told Longarm. "We don't intend to leave Oak Creek. We came here in good faith. We will stay here regardless."

Longarm nodded. It was a good thing he was sitting opposite the bed from where Monroe was standing. He was still struggling to get the heel of his left foot seated down inside his boot. Alex could see what he was doing and seemed to be having some difficulty in keeping herself from bursting out in guffaws.

If this shit kept up, Longarm thought, he was going to start feeling like a damn teenage kid again. Caught in the loft with sprigs of hay all over the backside of a pretty girl's skirt.

The worst part of it was that if Monroe caught on and went to screaming there wasn't much Longarm would be able to do about it. He couldn't fight back if a man was only wanting to protect his daughter's honor. Hell of a situation for a grown man to get himself into, though.

The heel of his foot slid the rest of the way down to where it belonged, and he felt a whole lot better.

"Just so you and the rest of the folks know," Longarm said, "I got no orders about running anybody off government land. I don't figure to invent none either. Just like I told you all yesterday. That hasn't changed from anything any other deputy said or will say."

"Thank you." Monroe frowned. "Do you think . . . ?"

"Doesn't much matter what I think, Monroe. I'm not the one saying any of this stuff. And if it comes to that, Monroe, you fellas got to know that I won't stand up against another officer who's acting in the commission of his duties. I won't do that for you or anybody else."

Alex looked worried. It occured to Longarm that he hadn't ever quite gotten around to explaining anything to her about the meeting that had been going on across the street. But then they'd had other pressing matters to think about at the time.

Her father explained the situation briefly, and her worried frown got deeper. "Will we have to move again, Daddy?"

Monroe glanced at Longarm, then back to his daughter. "No," he said flatly. "This is where we put roots down, baby. This is where we stay."

Longarm hoped the man was telling Alex no lie. But then this wasn't any of his affair, as Lew Campbell had made damn well clear.

Custis Long already had his plate full with the fake Billy Two and the unknown ambusher with the bow and arrows.

Chapter 20

Longarm declined an invitation from Monroe Dyche that he stay for supper with Monroe and Alex. It was one thing—and a fine one at that—to pass pleasant hours romping a man's daughter. It was something else again to sit across the table and make small talk with the same man whose daughter had just been initiated into the ways of womanhood.

"Reckon I'll see if I can learn anything across the street instead," Longarm said. "But I do thank you." He gave Alex a wink that her father couldn't see. The girl beamed. She looked quite healthy now despite the wound she had suffered earlier. In fact, Longarm doubted she had looked this glowingly cheerful in years. If ever. Monroe, fortunately, didn't seem to notice.

The shopkeeper led Longarm out of Alex's bedroom to the tiny kitchen that was included in the living quarters he had built behind his store.

"Alex seems awfully fond of you, Longarm," Monroe said. But without any signs of anxiety or anger.

"She's a mighty fine girl," Longarm told the proud father. "And I really think she's gonna be just fine now. I'll, uh, check on her from time to time. If that's all right with you."

"I'd appreciate it," Monroe said, not realizing he was inviting the fox into the henhouse for repeat visits. "Would you like to see some of her work?"

"Pardon me?"

"Her work. Her paintings. You know."

"Oh. Sure." Longarm gave the man a smile that was more politeness than real interest. He had quite forgotten Alex Dyche's would-be career as an artist. It was her interest in photography that brought them together to begin with, not her paintings.

"I built her a sunroom out back here, like a studio, where she can work." Monroe sounded papa-proud, and Longarm resigned himself to wasting a few minutes while Monroe showed off what his little girl could do.

The "sunroom" was a lean-to attached to the rear of the store building. The room faced an alley and vacant lot. Which was immediately, almost overwhelmingly apparent because so much of the wall and roof area was made of glass instead of wood. It must have cost Monroe a bundle to have so much plate glass shipped into a town as remote as Oak Creek.

As a studio it did make sense, though. The whole interior of the small work space was flooded with light even this late in the afternoon.

Pots and jars and cans littered shelving that had been built onto the solid wall between the studio and the shop. Those, Longarm figured, judging from the brightly colored smudges on their labels, contained pigments and oils and whatever the hell else. Stuff to mix up the paints Alex would need for her work.

A slightly wider counter held brushes and metal spatulas and nasty-smelling rags.

An easel standing near the wall of windows held a canvas-wrapped board or something, a piece that was maybe two by three feet in size, that was mostly empty except for a few pencil marks that hadn't yet begun to take any shape that Longarm could recognize. Work just begun, he figured.

It was all real interesting, he was sure, but...

"Here," Monroe said proudly. He was bending over a dozen or more of the canvas-covered boards that were held on a rack with their faces turned toward the wall. He examined them until he found one he wanted and then extracted it from the rest, turning proudly to show Longarm the front of the thing.

Alex's painting was... damn near breathtaking, Longarm admitted.

The girl wasn't some dab-and-daub amateur who was playing at being an artist.

She was *good*.

The scene her proud daddy was showing off was a sunrise over the arid, ugly plains.

Except the way Alex had painted it, the barren stretch of near desert wasn't ugly at all.

She'd managed to catch the gold and pink glow of the rising sun so that the scene looked fresh and alive and filled with the promise of the day that was dawning.

And the color and shadow she showed on the land made it seem rugged on the surface but promising too. Like a man could bring cattle or crops to this raw land and have it grow into something good.

Longarm thought he recognized, actually recognized, Horse Butte, although from a different angle from the one Longarm had seen when Amos Vent brought him up here.

And over there was a swale he remembered crossing, except in Alex's picture the contours of the land were shaped different from what was real, the changes she'd made somehow making the picture more alive and inviting and pretty. That little change shaped the way the eye was drawn along the landscape and took the emphasis off Horse Butte and put it on the gold-toned land under the dawning sun.

"Son of a bitch," Longarm blurted.

Monroe grinned.

"She's good," he added. "Mighty good."

Monroe's grin expanded and so did his chest.

"Picture like that oughta be in a museum or one of them ... what do you call them? ... gallery places. Oughta be hung where folks can see it, anyhow."

Monroe beamed and preened under the praise for his only child. "Wait. I thought you'd like that one. But wait until you see this." He set the Horse Butte landscape aside and dug into the pile of unframed canvases for another selection. And then another after that.

One by one Longarm oohed and ahhed and admired the paintings Monroe held up for him to see.

And there wasn't a one of them that he had to lie about when he voiced his admiration for Alex's artwork.

The girl was a by-damn genuine artist, not just a drawer of pictures.

Longarm was impressed and didn't at all mind the delay at getting back across the street.

"Thank you," he told Monroe when he had viewed, and thoroughly enjoyed, every one of Alex's canvases. The thanks were no lie at all.

Monroe replaced the canvases the way Alex had left them and trailed Longarm to the front of the shop building. "We'll see you later, Longarm. Come by any time."

"I'll do that, Monroe. Tell Alex good-bye for me again, please." He turned and headed across the street toward Merle Dyche's saloon and hotel, his stomach reminding him that it would soon be suppertime.

Chapter 21

Supper was a lonely affair. Amos Vent and Deputy Campbell hadn't come back yet—and might not return at all if Campbell had it in mind to try and track the supposed Billy Mann away from Oak Creek—and the men who were still in Merle's place weren't particularly friendly this evening toward one of the federal officers who might be throwing them out of their new homes.

Last night everyone had been eager to help him. Now they shifted as far away from Longarm as they could get and kept their voices low so he couldn't overhear.

That was the sort of thing any lawman has to get used to as a part of his job. But Longarm wouldn't say it was a part of the job that he particularly liked.

Even Merle Dyche wasn't interested in jawing with him this evening, but hung out with some of his townspeople chums at the far end of the bar.

Longarm took his time about eating anyway. A fella couldn't spend himself fretting about others' fears and prejudices. Then he leaned back and ordered a glass of rye to cut the grease off the meal he'd just eaten.

He fired up a cheroot, tasted the rye . . . and decided that the bartender had given good advice when he said a man should avoid the stuff that passed for rye whiskey in Oak Creek. It was something south of being merely awful.

On the other hand, bad rye is better than none. Longarm took a swallow, crossed his boots at the ankles and let the meal settle in his whiskey-warmed belly. He . . .

He sat up straighter in his chair and strained to listen. There was something, a low, murmuring, babbling kind of sound, that he thought he could hear outdoors somewhere.

A moment later the other men in the place caught it too and stopped their talking, making it easier for everybody to listen.

Somewhere outside there were voices being raised. Angry voices. Curses. Threats?

Longarm was on his feet and moving, the rest of his drink forgotten behind him and his cheroot clamped between his teeth. Mayor Dyche and the other men hurried to try and keep up with him.

There was a disturbance on the street, all right.

Down the block in the direction of the burned-out photography studio a small crowd had gathered in the last traces of twilight.

The focus of their attention seemed to be Deputy Marshal Lew Campbell, who sat his horse in the middle of the Oak Creek crowd. Being on horseback he stood tall among the men who crowded around his nervous, head-tossing mount. There was no sign of Amos Vent now, although the two men had ridden out of town together.

Longarm legged it down the street in a hurry and came up behind the men, who were all paying attention to Campbell.

"I gave you fair warning," Campbell was saying. "Now I'm placing you under arrest. Every stinking one of you land jumpers."

There must have been sixteen, eighteen men already in the street, and more were coming. And Campbell was putting all of them under arrest? By himself?

The man sure had a smooth and silky way about him, Longarm figured. Calculated to win friends and charm snakes.

"You hear me, you sons of bitches? All of you. Under arrest. This minute." Campbell's voice was loud. But to give him credit it wasn't shaky. Not the least lick. The man had sand even if he was short on sense.

"You can't tell us what to do," someone protested in a shout. "We have our rights too. And you don't have no warrants for us. We have our rights here."

"Damn right you do. You got the right to die where you stand if you don't do what I tell you," Campbell threatened.

"But you—"

"I gave you a lawful order," Campbell interrupted. "You failed to obey it. Now you're under arrest."

Longarm frowned. The way Billy Vail always taught it, "lawful" was what a court said it was. Until or unless a court of law said something was lawful, the deputy was kinda hung out on his own, although an application of common sense would usually see things through to where they ought to be.

"Fuck you," somebody shouted from the edge of the crowd.

Campbell's head jerked and his eyes narrowed as he searched the crowd to see who had hollered. But every face in sight was no doubt hard-set and hostile.

"Fuck you," somebody else shouted from the other side of the crowd.

Crowd, Longarm thought. They were right now. But these men had a look about them that said the crowd could turn into a mob right quick if the cards happened to fall that way.

Probably the only thing keeping them from it now was the fact that most of these fellows were from the East, where folks tended to take the law more serious than many did out here. Western men sometimes found it easier to handle their own brand of lawing than to look to somebody else for it.

Unfortunately, though, those first few trial shouts were already showing these boys that they could cuss a deputy and get away with it.

And they might not realize that there were limits to what a salty deputy like this one might want to stand for.

"Fuck you," another man hollered at the back of Lew Campbell's head.

Campbell looked in that direction.

"Fuck you" a new voice shouted behind him.

"Fuck you."

Campbell scowled. One of his Colts appeared in his fist.

Campbell was worried now, Longarm could see. The pissed-off men of Oak Creek had him and his horse ringed in tight, the townspeople drawn in on all sides so that Campbell wouldn't be able to break out from among them if anybody had sense enough to grab a rein and hang on.

It was one thing for the men of Oak Creek to get scared. It would be a damn disaster, though, if Campbell panicked.

If there was anything Oak Creek didn't need now it was a bloodbath. No matter who it was that was supplying the blood.

"Back off, you assholes," Campbell screamed. His voice was shrill, right on the edge of spilling across into fear. He pointed his revolver toward the sky and fired a shot.

Instead of having a chilling effect on the men, though, the noise only seemed to agitate them all the further. They muttered and pushed closer to the mounted deputy in their middle.

Campbell's horse tried to rear at the sound, but someone grabbed the cheekpiece of Campbell's bridle and hauled the animal's head down.

"Let go, you son of a bitch. Let go." Campbell chopped down with the barrel of his pistol, and the man holding onto his horse reeled backward with his scalp bloody. Campbell looked like he was going to shoot, but his horse came onto its hind legs, pawing and snorting, and the gun discharged into the air a second time.

Longarm was already busy bulling his way through the mass of bodies that pressed close around Campbell and his horse.

"Move aside, boys. Step aside now, thank you." Longarm kept his voice calm and sure as he waded through the crowd like a swimmer trying to make headway in a spill of molasses. "Move away, please. That's right. Move aside."

"Calm down, Lew. Ease off here." He grabbed a rein and brought the trembling, suddenly sweaty horse back down onto all fours.

"What the fuck are you doing here, Long?" Campbell snarled.

So much for gratitude, Longarm thought with a patient smile. "You want I should go back and finish my drink, Lew?"

Campbell blinked. "I got this under control," he hissed. He tried to keep his voice low, but probably every man in the near-mob heard it anyhow.

"I know you do," Longarm lied, "but one deputy has to back another, right?" He turned to the men who were standing nearby.

"Go home," he told them calmly. "Everybody go home now. The excitement's over for tonight."

"That fucker tried to arrest us, Marshal," someone protested.

"Yes, but it's only a house arrest." Longarm thought quickly, trying to recall the man's name. "You're under a sort of house arrest, Howard. That's a formality. Until the courts sort this through and decide who's right here. You don't actually have to leave, and the deputy and I aren't actually going to put you in irons. Deputy Marshal Campbell is only trying to start the formalities so the courts can decide who has the right to be here and who doesn't."

That was all a line of the purest bullshit. Longarm made it up as he went along. The important thing was that while he was saying it he was smiling and nodding and making it *sound* like it just might possibly be so.

"I know you want this to be resolved, Howard. I know you don't want any cloud hanging over you here. So why don't you boys cooperate with the deputy and me."

"He coulda *said* that's what he was doin'," somebody grumbled.

"And so he would've if you'd given him a chance," Longarm pleasantly lied yet again. "Now you boys all drift back to your homes, why don't you. And remember, fellas, technically you're all under house arrest. You're not to leave Oak Creek until this is sorted through." Longarm was smiling and nodding agreeably. And hoping like hell that no one realized just yet that what Custis Long was telling them—which was that they weren't allowed to leave until a court considered their problem—was just exactly the opposite of what Deputy Campbell had been telling them, which was to get the hell out and do it right now.

Longarm smiled and bobbed his head and made a shooing motion toward the men standing closest to him.

He didn't think it would take all that much persuasion to get them to disband. After all, none of them would particularly want to be shot, and there had already been a couple loud noises made.

Best of all, the mob mood that had begun to sweep through them had dissipated by now and each of them would be able to think.

A mob is one scary damn thing, almost like a composite being that has a single, frightening mentality of its own. A mob knows that it can claw apart any man no matter how well he is armed. But then a mob doesn't give a shit about how many individual members of it have to get shot down in that process.

Once the men in a mob become a crowd again it starts to dawn on them that *they* might be one of the unlucky ones that gets shot in the process. Once they have a moment to realize that they aren't so intent on trouble come what may.

Longarm smiled and shooed them back a few paces. Then

a few paces more, and the men on the fringes of the crowd began to turn their backs and walk away.

Longarm let out a sigh of relief as the last of them turned their backs.

"I had it under control," Campbell complained.

Longarm stared up at the man in complete disbelief. He didn't know whether he ought to laugh. Or cuss.

He decided the best course would be to pretend he hadn't heard.

"Buy you a drink, Deputy?"

Campbell grunted and shoved his Colt back into its holster. He stepped down off his horse and retrieved its rein from Longarm's hand.

Chapter 22

Merle Dyche served drinks to the two deputies but not with what you would call enthusiasm or welcome. The mayor scowled as he set out two shots of his poorest bar whiskey. Longarm had asked for rye, but the request was ignored and the drinks poured from the handiest container of rotgut. He got the impression that Dyche's bartender wouldn't have been willing to do even that much for Deputy Marshal Lew Campbell. Dyche compounded the insult by refusing to accept money from either deputy. There wasn't any way Longarm—or presumably Campbell either—could mistake the gesture for generosity.

At least on the surface of things Campbell seemed happily oblivious to the whole thing. He downed his shot and smacked his lips loudly, seemingly unaware that the other customers in the saloon were clustered as far away from the officers as they could get.

"That's good," Campbell said in the general direction of the backbar mirror. "Another." He slapped his shot glass down on the bar. And was ignored by both the mayor and the bartender, both of whom were pretending to be busy elsewhere.

"Where's Amos?" Longarm asked, trying to keep Campbell from getting his feathers ruffled once he finally figured out that he was being snubbed.

"Said something about having to get back down to Coldwater," Campbell said. "Son of a bitch split off on me middle of the afternoon, he did."

Longarm kept his expression neutral as he tasted the raw liquor Merle had poured for him—the stuff was even worse than Merle's cheap version of rye—but couldn't help recollecting that Ranger Vent had said his assignment here was to hold Deputy Campbell's hand and help the federal man out any way the Texas Rangers could.

Amos didn't have any other job he had to run back to Texas for. He was just sliding clear of Campbell, Longarm was pretty sure.

The feisty little man standing at Longarm's side—somewhere just south of his shoulder level actually—sure was one for making friends.

Campbell banged his glass on the bar a few more times, keeping it up until he finally got a response from Merle and a surly refill. The deputy laid a quarter on the bar. Merle turned and walked away from it.

"You don't want another?"

"No, thanks." Longarm would about as soon ask for a shot of mule piss as another of those.

"You!" Campbell called loudly.

The mayor turned and gave him a surly look. Campbell beckoned him close again. Dyche stood where he was but at least had the courtesy to pay attention.

"I need a room tonight," Campbell declared.

"Full up," Merle said, not even trying to make it sound like it was the truth.

"Damn," Campbell muttered. "I sure was looking forward to a bed tonight." He shook his head and turned his attention to the shot glass of atrocious whiskey.

Longarm could hardly believe it. Unless Campbell was

one hell of an actor, the little deputy from Fort Smith had absolutely no idea that he was unwelcome here. Incredible. But it sure looked to be true.

The polite and decent thing for Longarm to do, of course, would be to tell Campbell that he could bunk in with Longarm in his hotel room.

He glanced toward Merle Dyche, who was looking at Longarm like he was waiting for just that.

Longarm gave Merle a hidden smile and a quick wink that Campbell couldn't see. The tension went out of Merle's shoulders after that, and he turned and began talking to the townfolk down at that end of the bar.

"Saw a good camping spot," Campbell was saying. "Not too far from one of the wells. We'll set up there."

It was a good thing Longarm wasn't in the process of trying to choke down any of Merle's rotgut at the time. He would have sprayed it all over himself.

Shit, he'd been looking forward to a good bed tonight too. And in fact had one already fixed up and paid for. Now Campbell was blithely assuming that he was in command here and that the deputy from Denver would just naturally be joining him.

Longarm looked at Merle again and sighed. He didn't want to get anything more started, dammit. Better to keep his mouth shut and make a rocky bed while his room went empty for the night.

"Whatever you say, Lew," Longarm said pleasantly.

The campsite really could have been worse. It was just down the slope from one of the tall, creaking windmills that supplied the town with water. Campbell and Longarm laid their bedrolls out in the soft sand at the edge of the dry wash that could be called a creek only by those who were awful optimistic or by those who had a fine sense of humor.

They'd eaten at Merle's place before they sought out the camping place, so there was no need for a fire. In particular since Longarm was in no mood to sit up late in the night sharing confidences and small talk with Lew Campbell.

"You want to play some cards or something, Long?"

"Naw, I'm kinda bushed. Think I'll turn in now."

Campbell smirked. "Fella with no more stamina than that couldn't make it working out of Fort Smith, Long. We're salty. Not like the crew that fat boss of yours runs." He snorted.

Longarm gave the asshole a dark look but bit back the things he might have said.

Fat boss, huh. Billy Vail? Billy Vail or any one of his deputies could run this Campbell into the ground and not break a sweat doing it.

Still, the little son of a bitch was a U.S. deputy marshal.

It would've been bad manners to poke a .44–40 up his left nostril.

And a fistfight with a prick that small wouldn't hardly be fair either.

Longarm grunted and wrapped himself up tight inside his bedroll.

If he couldn't go to sleep right away—and he was much too pissed to be sleepy—he could at least pretend so Campbell would shut up and quit making things worse.

Chapter 23

The sound of the windmill lazily turning on the evening breeze was a comforting sort of thing. Slow and soft and rhythmic. It soothed a man and made his cares seem smaller.

A few feet away the rough-and-ready old boy from Fort Smith was already snoring so hard it was a wonder his mustache stayed in place on his lip. Longarm shifted deeper into his blankets—it was becoming cool now—and thought about getting some sleep himself.

He would've rather slipped over to see Alex Dyche again. But her father was no doubt at home and likely wouldn't favor the idea of his wounded daughter walking out in the evening for a bit of belly bumping. Just thinking about Alex with her eagerness and energy was enough to give Longarm a hard-on under his blankets. That kind of thought wasn't going to do much to help put him to sleep, so he tried not to think about it.

Naturally, human nature having a habit of being perverse whenever a chance arises, trying *not* to think about something is pretty much the same as telling yourself that that is precisely what you are *going* to be thinking about.

Longarm lay there getting hornier and hornier the more he tried to avoid remembering how Alex felt when she was wrapped tight around him with that rounded little ass humping and her breath coming quick and ragged in his ear.

This was *not* helping, dammit. It . . .

The wind slacked off and then died altogether. The vanes and gears of the windmill creaked to a halt, and the sound of water jetting softly into the tank slowed to a stop.

Longarm smiled to himself. Some nights were like that, sad to say. Some just seemed longer than others.

Now he didn't even have the comforting noises from the mill to keep him company.

The silence that swept in now was deep. From far away he heard a yip of laughter. Somewhere else there was the dull thump of a window sash being shut. Alex's bedroom window came to mind, and he shifted from one shoulder to the other, trying to gouge a more comfortable hollow in the sand under his ground cloth.

A woman's voice was briefly raised. Something about no-good drunks staying out to all hours. Longarm smiled a little in the night. Poor liquored-up son of a bitch was catching it from the old woman.

His slight smile turned into a frown as the new-fallen stillness brought him another sound. A scrape of something—leather?—on sand? There was a momentary pause, then the tiny hint of sound was repeated. And again.

Longarm's eyes snapped open, and he slid the big Thunderer out of his holster. He hadn't stripped for bed when he had turned in, mostly because he hadn't actually expected to be able to sleep for a while. He hadn't even taken his gun belt off. The Colt came into his hand under the cover of his blankets, and he slowed his breathing so he could listen more closely.

Footsteps? He thought so. Forty, fifty yards away. About where the water tank and windmill were.

Somebody might just be coming down to the well to fetch home a bucket of water.

Longarm didn't believe that for a minute.

A townsman drawing water wouldn't be moving sneaky about it.

This guy was trying to walk without making any noise. He took a step, paused, took another, paused again.

Longarm wouldn't have thought anything strange about a man out walking by the well.

But this?

He shifted position again, drawing his knees up ready to spring out from under the bedroll.

He switched the Colt to his left hand for a moment and reached out to fumble on the ground. There weren't any rocks or pebbles close to hand so he settled for a bit of sand instead, flipping it backhanded toward the sleeping Fort Smith deputy.

Campbell snorted and rolled over in his sleep. Longarm tossed another spray of fine grit onto him. Campbell's snoring quit, and he came awake.

"What? What is it?"

His voice was unnaturally loud in the stillness.

Off toward the mill the sounds of the stealthy footsteps quit.

Longarm rolled his eyes. Dumb SOB. He transferred the Colt back into his right hand and held himself tense and poised.

"What is it?" Campbell repeated. "D'you wake me or something?" He threw off his bedroll and stood.

If somebody out there had hostile intentions, Campbell was making this awful easy. He was silhouetted dark against the starlit backdrop of the night sky, at least from Longarm's level.

"Down," Longarm hissed under his breath. The Fort Smith man either didn't hear or chose to ignore the warning.

Campbell wasn't armed, Longarm saw. He had left his brace of guns under his saddle when he stood up.

Damned if he didn't stumble clear of the bedrolls and walk a dozen paces in the direction of the windmill.

He'd already loosened his trousers when he went to bed. Now he flopped his dong out and took a long piss, sighing with the pleasure of it as he finished and tucked himself back into his drawers.

Longarm was trying to concentrate on the shadows where the sounds might have originated.

He could see nothing now. Could hear nothing.

If there had been anyone there—and he damn sure wasn't certain that there had been—well, the guy must have slipped away by now.

Thank you very much, Deputy Campbell, Longarm thought sourly.

Cameron hawked loudly and spat.

"Shit," Longarm mumbled.

"What's that?" Campbell finally remembered that he wasn't alone and turned.

"Nothing," Longarm said. "Nothing important."

Campbell grunted.

Longarm pushed the blankets back and got to his feet, stifling a yawn. It had probably been nothing anyway. But as long as he was awake he might as well take a look over there by the mill. Just to be sure.

"Wonder what the hell it was woke me up," Campbell complained.

At the same moment, the sound of it almost masked by Campbell's chatter, Longarm heard a faint, twanging sound.

Before he had time to react he felt a blow in his midsection like somebody had punched him in the gut. But not particularly hard. A playful kind of punch.

Except this wasn't playful!

He felt the arrow hit him and felt more than heard the flutter of its feathers. He heard a distinct crack as the wooden shaft broke.

Longarm was already in motion, doubling over, falling to the side with his Colt extended.

118

A shadow near the base of the water tank moved, and he snapped a shot at it.

He hit *something* over there. He could hear the thump of the flat-nosed lead slug striking home. But there was no scream, no grunt of pain, no thud of a body falling.

"What the shit!" Campbell flung himself facedown in the sand and began crawling back toward his bedroll and the guns he'd left there.

"Get down, dammit."

Campbell was between Longarm and the water tank. Longarm moved to the side, popped high onto his knees and triggered another round into the shadows where he thought the bowman was.

Campbell came up in a rush, threw himself past Longarm and sprawled onto his bedroll grabbing for his guns.

Over by the water tank there was . . . nothing.

No noise. No movement. Nothing at all.

Campbell had his guns by now. He stayed low, the muzzle of his Colt searching the darkness just as Longarm's was.

But neither of them had anything to shoot at now.

The bow-and-arrow ambusher was gone.

"Son of a bitch," Longarm snapped. He motioned Campbell to the left while he moved right. The two deputies bellied forward with their guns ready. But by then both of them knew there would be nothing for them to shoot at.

The man was gone.

Longarm paused, letting Campbell complete the search without him.

It occurred to Longarm that he'd been shot in the gut. But he felt no pain.

He'd always heard that a properly sharp arrowhead causes little pain. But this was ridiculous.

He felt of his stomach.

There was the splintered arrow shaft, all right. What little was left of it after it broke off. There was a stub of wood maybe three, four inches long.

Longarm traced the shaft closer with his fingers. And grinned.

The arrow had hit him dead center. Fortunately. The arrowhead was buried now in the double fold of leather inside his belt buckle. He felt behind the buckle. There was no sharp tip protruding through the bottom layer of belt leather. The tongue of his belt or maybe parts of the buckle itself had stopped the point and left it embedded in his gun belt.

Luck. It could come in handy. An archer couldn't hit a target the size of a belt buckle on purpose one time out of ten, probably. This guy's shot had been just that true. And just that lucky, lucky at least from Longarm's point of view.

"There's nobody here," Campbell called from beside the water tank. "But you sure hell hit what you aimed at."

"What?"

"You shot the water tank, you dumbfuck," Campbell said. "Put two holes in it knee high, Long. Got a hell of a stream started over here." He laughed and slapped his thigh. "Just wait till I tell the boys back in Fort Smith what scares you Denver farts. Yessirree, Long. You done shot you a water tank that was creeping up on you in the night."

Sure. The kind of water tank that uses a bow and arrows to shoot back with.

Longarm shook his head and considered whether he should beat the crap out of Lew Campbell. Or just quietly pity the man instead.

He settled for prizing the arrowhead out of his belt buckle and tucking the thing into a shirt pocket.

There seemed no point in showing it to Campbell.

Even if the Fort Smith deputy was capable of understanding—and that was certainly subject to question—it wouldn't change anything.

The man was simply too dense to be worth trying to educate.

Longarm bent and began to roll his bedding. Now that the bowman had them spotted it didn't seem a good idea to hang around and offer the guy seconds.

Chapter 24

Longarm hunkered down on the hard ground beside the patch of dark mud his bullets had created last night. Water continued to trickle out of the lower hole in the galvanized steel of the water tank while high overhead the vanes of the windmill rotated, pumping the sucker rod monotonously up and down but barely able to keep pace with the water that was being lost.

On his way over here this morning Longarm had stopped behind a half-sod, half-lumber house and swiped two thumb-sized scraps off the owner's firewood pile.

Now he was squatting in the sunlight and using his knife to whittle plugs to stop up the .44 caliber holes in the water tank.

He'd gone and made the mess so it was his place to fix it. It seemed a fair enough trade-off. Better two holes in this water tank than one in his belly.

He had no idea where Deputy Campbell had wandered off to after daylight. Didn't particularly give a shit either. Out of sight was quite good enough for the time being.

Besides, as long as the Fort Smith deputy was nosing around Oak Creek looking for a direction to take, he wasn't in Denver getting closer to William Mann's hideout in Longarm's boardinghouse.

Just thinking about that was enough to make a fella nervous. The attorney general would howl like a dog on a moonlit night if it ever came out that a fugitive from federal warrants was being kept hidden in a deputy marshal's room. And at a U.S. marshal's suggestion, at that.

Wouldn't that make for a fine howdydoo.

So probably it was better after all to have Campbell sniffing around in Oak Creek rather than out where he might actually accomplish something.

Between those two, though, the choice was a hard one.

Longarm grunted and examined the plug he'd just carved. It looked right to the eye. He fitted it into the lower bullet hole and encountered resistance. Perfect. He smacked it with his palm to drive the wood into the small round hole. The trickle of escaping water stopped immediately. Give the wood time to soften and swell, and the tank would be effectively sealed again. Longarm picked up the second wood scrap and started on the other plug. Likely he could get that one finished before the mill pumped the water up to that level again.

The whittling was dull and mechanical, giving him plenty of time to think while his hands were busy.

After only a moment he blinked and stopped what he was doing.

What the hell?

It hadn't especially occurred to him last night.

Now it hit him at least as hard as that arrow out of the darkness had.

The bowman had shot at Longarm. But *not* at Lew Campbell.

Why?

Longarm stood, his feet planted very close to where that son of a bitch with the bow had been standing last night when he fired.

He stared down toward the dry creekbed to the spot where his bedroll had been and where Campbell's had been. He tried to reconstruct in his mind just exactly where each of them had been when the bowman made his shot.

Campbell had been there, standing up on his hind legs, and from this spot would have been clearly visible even in the night.

He'd been a good ten paces closer to the bowman than Longarm. He'd just finished taking a leak and was right there in plain sight.

Yet the bowman hadn't fired until Longarm stood up too, convinced by Campbell's unmolested piss that he'd been mistaken about hearing footsteps here by the well.

And when the guy shot, he didn't shoot at Campbell, who would have been much, much easier to hit.

He fired *past* Deputy Lew Campbell and *at* Deputy Custis Long.

Now why the *fuck* would an ambusher want to do that?

Both officers would be seen as a threat to any fugitive among the townspeople of Oak Creek.

Both of them were here—at least so far as anybody this side of Denver knew—to arrest the same William Mann on charges of land fraud and murder.

Both of them carried the exact same badges and authority.

And for that matter, it was the Fort Smith deputy and not Longarm who would have a clear lock on the title if anybody wanted to take a vote in Oak Creek and decide on the town's most unpopular male human.

So why in hell would the guy with the bow pass up an easy shot at Deputy Campbell and wait for a harder one at Custis Long?

Longarm scowled and went so far as to walk down to where his bedroll had been last night and look at the scene again in the daytime.

The different perspective didn't change a thing about what he already knew.

Campbell would have been a *much* surer shot for the guy with the bow.

And he'd passed it up to try for Longarm instead.

That just purely wasn't a logical thing for anybody to do. *Given the facts as Longarm knew them.*

He grunted softly to himself and reconsidered.

If a person, any person, law abiding or criminal it don't matter which, does something, anything at all, then that thing is perfectly logical and reasonable and the right thing to do insofar as he himself sees the situation.

That right there is one of the basic facts of humankind that any lawman learns early in the game.

Nobody does something that *he* thinks is crazy. Not even if he is crazy as hell. To *him* it all seems right and proper. Regardless how somebody else might think to look at it.

So if Longarm figured this business last night to be unreasonable based on what he knew, well, the truth then was that he didn't know all the facts involved here.

Something was missing.

Something didn't fit.

That man with the bow shot at Longarm and not at Campbell for a *reason*.

Even though Longarm hadn't the faintest idea what that reason could possibly be.

He grunted again and began to savagely rip at the stub of wood in his hand, slicing and gouging at the plug as a way of working off the sudden sense of frustration that had come over him.

Did somebody in this town have a mad on for Custis Long personally, irrespective of the fact that he just happened to be a U.S. deputy marshal?

Longarm tried to think again about all the folks he'd seen since he came to the town.

There wasn't a one of them he recalled ever having seen before in his life. Certainly there weren't any old, half-forgotten enemies among them. And Longarm wasn't exactly the sort of man to let old enemies completely slip his mind. A relative of an old enemy then? Almost anything was possible. He sighed. Sure. But possibilities weren't what he needed here. What he needed was some truth, dammit.

Why hadn't that guy shot at Campbell?

"Shit," Longarm grumbled.

"Longarm?"

He looked up, his scowl fading and quickly replaced with a welcoming smile.

Alex Dyche was coming toward the well from the direction of her studio at the back of her father's store.

"Good morning, Longarm. Somebody said they saw you coming this way. I . . . hoped I'd find you here."

She was wearing the usual duster and gloves and deeply hooded bonnet that she favored when she was out in public. But he thought she was awfully pretty regardless, even knowing about the scars those garments hid. There was a hell of a lot more to this girl than the surface.

Longarm smiled and moved up the slope to meet her.

Chapter 25

Alex had sought him out this morning, yet she seemed shy again seeing him, or to be more accurate, being seen by him, in the daylight, he suspected.

Not that she'd been at all shy in her bedroom yesterday, but here in public that seemed to have changed. She kept her head down and her eyes toward the ground. Longarm tipped her chin up so he could see under the hood of her bonnet. He smiled at her and said, "I'd grab you and kiss you but I wouldn't want to embarrass you was anybody looking this way."

The warmth of Alex's smile and the sudden leap of joy into her pale eyes was enough to tell him that he'd figured it right. She hadn't been sure he wouldn't reject her today after taking her virginity yesterday.

"I don't care if you don't," she ventured.

Longarm grinned and took her into his arms. He pushed the cloth of the bonnet out of the way and examined the inside of her mouth with his tongue. He could feel Alex sag and go limp against him as her knees turned rubbery, and her breath quickened in immediate response to the touch of his body against hers.

"Is there someplace we could go?" she whispered. "Someplace private?"

"I have a room. But it's, uh, in your uncle's place. I don't much think he'd like me taking you in there and closing the door."

"Uncle Merle would have a fit. And Daddy is in the store. He'd hear if we tried to sneak into my room." She giggled. "We could use the studio except then everybody in the whole town could watch."

"Maybe not such a good idea, huh?"

"No. All the ladies would be jealous and then I'd have to fight them for you."

"Flattering, but . . ." He laughed.

"You could ride with me. I could say I want to go out and make some sketches. I was going to anyway."

"I'd like to Alex, but I got work to do here."

"I know. I . . . want to talk to you about something anyway. It might help if you want a picture of Mr. Mann."

"Really?"

"We could talk about it on the way. But only if you agree to go with me while *I* work."

"You realize of course that blackmail of a peace officer is a federal offense, don't you?"

Alex giggled. "I'll willingly submit, Officer."

"Kinda hard to discourage, aren't you?"

"Kind of anxious to feel you inside me again," she said.

"I reckon I could go with you." He looked around at the small, sunbaked town. "I can't say as I'm accomplishing all that much today anyhow."

"I'll go get my sketch pads and tell Daddy where I'll be. I'll pick you up right here, dear."

"Pick me up?"

"I have a little cart that Daddy lets me use. I won't be but a few minutes. Promise."

"I'll wait for you here then."

Alex hurried away, and Longarm quickly finished the second plug for the leaky water tank.

The girl knew the country around Oak Creek probably better than anyone. And no wonder. Longarm could recognize much of what they passed from the landscape scenes Monroe had shown him in her studio yesterday. He was amazed that Alex was able to find so much beauty in a land so dry and seemingly empty. Yet looking at it now the way her vision had shown it to him in her paintings he could see the truth of what she put onto her canvases. It was all there. A person only had to be willing to see it.

She'd been driving only fifteen or twenty minutes when she turned the little two-wheeled cart toward a stand of gray stunted cottonwoods that were managing to survive in a bend of the dry creekbed.

"This what you had in mind?" he asked.

"It isn't what I wanted to sketch today, actually. That's a mile or so farther up. But I thought, if you're interested, I mean, I thought we might stop here for a few minutes. This spot is shady. And private?" Alex sounded unsure again, like at any minute she expected him to make a face and tell her he wasn't interested in her body.

Longarm gave her a hug and hopped down off the cart as it came to a halt. He tethered the light driving horse to a cottonwood branch and lifted Alex down to the ground. Once there he continued to hold her, kissing her thoroughly until he felt her knees give way again. If that didn't convince her...

"Whew!" she said happily when he finally let go of her.

"I agree." He grinned.

Alex, incredibly, began to cry.

"What've I done now?"

"It isn't...it isn't you," she blubbered. "It's just... you're so handsome and fine. And I'm so...so..."

He kissed her again and this time his hand found her breast, kneading the soft flesh and making her gasp.

He picked her up and carried her the few paces down

128

into the shade of the runty cottonwoods, then lowered her gently onto the sloping bank where a few wisps of dry grass grew.

"You don't have to," she protested.

"That's all right. Long as I'm still allowed to want to." He reached for the buttons that held the duster closed high on her neck.

"If you'd rather, dear, I could just . . . you know . . . lift my skirt."

"What turned you so damn silly this morning?" He began stripping cloth away from her. Duster, gloves, bonnet and dress, until she was naked beside him.

Her scars seemed even more prominent in the harsh light of the morning sun, and Alex turned her face away from him. Longarm smiled and drew her chin back toward him. "Will you please quit worrying about things that don't matter."

Alex was crying again, but this time she didn't seem the least lick miserable. She began tugging and fumbling at his clothes. In less than a minute they were both naked in the shade-dappled sunlight.

"Yesterday. Didn't you tell me? That there are . . . more ways a woman can please a man? Things you haven't taught me yet?"

"Yes. If you for sure want to learn them."

"I want to," she said eagerly. "I want to do everything that will please you."

They were lying belly to belly, their faces only fractions of an inch apart. Longarm smiled and touched her lower lip with his fingertip. "Sure?"

"Positive."

He grinned and lightly ran the tip of his finger round and round the soft, smooth curve of her lip. Alex's eyes sagged nearly shut as she enjoyed the sensations of his touch.

He caressed her cheeks and eyes and went back to her lips, this time sliding his finger inside the warmth of her mouth.

"What you have to learn," he said, "is to just touch with your lips, not your teeth."

"Like this?"

"Mm-hum. And then you suck. In and out. Just like down here." With his other hand he probed gently into her vee, his finger finding its way through the patch of soft, curling hair there and sliding into her. Alex gasped.

"If you taste as good as you look..." Alex whispered.

She wriggled around so that her mouth was positioned close to him. He could feel the heat of her breath on his shaft.

"It's so pretty," she exclaimed.

And then she could talk no more, although she was able to gurgle and murmur quite happily as she learned another way to thoroughly please a man.

Longarm was willing to give as good as he got, and for the first time Alex discovered a woman's completion. Yesterday she had been too inexperienced to reach a full satisfaction. Today her body was ready for that final step. She shuddered and cried out, hips pumping and her vaginal lips pulsing and contracting as she spasmed in a deep, full climax.

"I didn't... I never knew anything could be like that, dear." There was awe and wonder in her voice now.

Longarm laughed. "You're a quick pupil, ma'am."

"But I haven't done anything for you yet. I mean, not really."

"I'd say we got time enough for that."

"We'll take time enough for that," she promised.

Alex bent to him again, her lips moist and warm. This time she was surer about what she was doing. And just as eager to do it.

"I *like* this," she said at one point, withdrawing an inch or so so she could speak.

"Well you don't have to sound so dang surprised about it," he said with a grin.

Alex laughed and pressed her cheek against him. "I'm so happy, Longarm. It was a terrible thing that brought you here. But I'm so glad that it did. Is it awful of me to say that, dear?"

"I don't know as it'd be a good idea for you to be repeating that where just anybody could hear. But I understand. To tell you the truth, I even agree."

He smiled and took her by the arm, drawing her up to face him and turning her onto her back.

"I'd be glad to finish you that way, dear," she offered. "I'd like to, really."

"Another time," he promised. "Right now, Alex, I want to be inside you." He raised himself over her, and Alex opened herself to him.

"Yes," she said. "Yes, please."

The girl was definitely a fine, quick learner.

Chapter 26

"Come to think of it," Longarm said, "haven't you forgotten something?" They were dressed and in the cart again as Alex drove them farther up the dry creek.

"I suppose I have at that, dear," She smiled. "I completely forgot to thank you. But I do. I truly do."

He laughed and kissed her. "Not that, dang it. You said you had something to tell me that might help me find this William Mann."

"Oh. I did forget, didn't I?" She gave him a peck on the cheek and guided the cart horse around a rocky outcrop. "Sorry. I, uh, was thinking about something else."

"And a fine something else it was, too. But don't tell me you not only blackmailed me, ma'am, you lied to do it."

"No, I really did think of something if you're wanting a picture of Mr. Mann."

"Well, I'm sure wanting a picture of the gentleman if you think there's someplace else one of those negative plates might've survived."

"Not a plate, dear. But I happened to remember last night . . . I was lying awake thinking about you, actually . . . and I happened to think that there just might be a photograph of Mr. Mann available."

Longarm sat upright on the hard bench seat, his interest in this possibility almost as high now as his interest in Alex Dyche undeniably was.

"Do you know anything about the Eastman process, dear?" Alex asked.

He shook his head.

"There is this man back East, I forget exactly where, who has developed a negative film process. He puts the emulsion onto celluloid film instead of glass."

"Like a shirt collar?"

"Sort of. But the celluloid is clear. And flexible. You can roll it up so that it fits into a small space. That way you don't have to use the plate holders and all the other paraphernalia that usually goes with the photographic processes. It is supposed to be really quite the coming thing."

"And this Maxwell had one of these film cameras?"

"Oh, no. Mr. Maxwell wouldn't have used anything like that. I'm told that the Eastman process is quite amateurish. It doesn't have the clarity of glass plates. The film is so small, for one thing. Mr. Maxwell would never have used it. But Mr. Warren's wife Ethel has an Eastman camera. She showed it to me. She wanted to be able to take pictures with it, snapshots she called them, to send to her family back East. And this Eastman camera seemed ideal for the purpose."

Longarm reached for a cheroot and cupped his hands around the match to light it.

"It's a terribly simple thing. Like a black box with a lens on the front and a shutter built right in and a crank to advance the roll of film from frame to frame. You just point the box at whatever you want a picture of and push down on this little lever thing, and the Eastman Company does all the rest. The box comes loaded with enough film for a hundred pictures. When you've used those all up, you mail the whole

133

camera back to the company. They develop your pictures and send them back to you along with another loaded camera."

"I'll be damned," Longarm said.

"I hope not. Anyway, Mrs. Warren was there the day they held the ceremony outside Uncle Merle's hotel."

"Did she...?"

"I'm not sure," Alex said, anticipating the question. "Ethel isn't sure herself, you see. I asked her about it this morning before I came looking for you. She remembers taking a number of pictures that day. But she can't remember for sure if she took any of Mr. Mann or not."

"Damn," Longarm said.

"She might have. She probably did. But we won't know for sure until those pictures are developed and returned."

"When should that be?" Longarm couldn't help being interested. If he could find photographic proof that the fellow who'd come here calling himself William Mann was *not* Billy Two...

"We don't know. Exactly."

Longarm raised an eyebrow in her direction.

"Ethel has never had one of those Eastman films developed and returned before. She just got the camera before they moved out here, you see, and she hasn't finished taking up her first film yet."

"You mean she hasn't even sent the box off to have it developed?"

"She still has twenty pictures or more to take," Alex said. "Of course she hasn't sent it off yet."

"But if it has to travel all the way back East..."

"Some place in New York state, I think."

"That could take weeks just to get there. Then however long more for this Eastman company to develop the pictures. And weeks more to get back here."

"I know." Alex sighed. "I suppose it wasn't such a helpful idea after all, was it."

Longarm hugged her. "It was a fine idea." He smiled. "Just an awful slow one."

Alex gave him a grin. "Surely that means you will have to wait here in Oak Creek until the film has been developed, dear." Her hand slid into his crotch to emphasize her meaning.

"I wish it did, Alex. Least as far as that's concerned. But I can't let a case drag on forever."

Normally, of course, there is no real time limit imposed on when a fugitive has to be collared.

In this case, though, Longarm and Billy Vail were fighting a clock of sorts. The longer the phony Mann situation went unresolved, the greater the danger to the real Billy Two. And the greater the danger that Billy One's involvement would be found out.

Longarm would hate like hell for Marshal Billy Vail to lose his job just because the mail service was so slow between No-Man's-Land and New York.

"I can't count on these pictures, Alex, but let's give them a try as a last resort sorta thing. Do you think this Mrs. Warren would send in the camera box early if I was to pay for it?"

"I could ask her. I'm pretty sure she would, dear."

"Let's give it a try then. Soon as we get back to town."

"I won't be long. There is the place I want to make my sketches."

She was pointing toward a rocky bank along the creekbed. It seemed every bit as dry and ugly as everything around it. Maybe even a little bit worse.

"Aw, c'mon. You can't find anything pretty to paint in that dreary mess."

Alex gave him an impish look and brought the cart to a stop. Her arrow wound from the day before wasn't slowing her down any. She was out of the cart and on the ground before he had time to come around and help her down. "Just wait. You'll see," she promised.

She led him to the top of the bank and pointed proudly downward into the bed of the sandy creek.

Longarm joined her. And realized then what she meant.

135

Hidden tight against the stone wall of the creek bank there was a tiny, emerald oasis of greenery.

The pocket of green couldn't have been more than twenty feet by ten and looked like some weird sort of mistake by which life had been picked up from someplace else and set down here in the midst of nothing.

There were lacy, delicate willows. Even a miniature, marshy basin filled with cattails and frogs and tadpoles. Lush, thick grass surrounded it. It was fed by a tiny spring that seeped out of the rock, collected briefly there to create the oasis and then disappeared into the dry sands of the creekbed they had been following ever since they left Oak Creek.

"Well, I'll be go to hell," Longarm said.

Alex acted as pleased as if she had invented the whole thing and was presenting it to him now as a gift.

And in a way perhaps she was.

"I found it just a few days ago. I thought about bringing you here to make love this morning. But I wanted to sketch it first. Before we, um, trample the grass. And whatever else." She giggled. "Come on. I'll show you the way down."

"Hold it."

Longarm's voice had gone cold and sharp. He grabbed her by the arm and hauled her roughly back away from the top of the bank.

"Dear!"

But Longarm's Colt was in his hand now, and he was motioning for her to stay back away from the edge.

Alex had just said she hadn't wanted to trample down the lush grass beside the tiny, hidden marsh.

But somebody damn sure had already.

The foliage showed signs of human intrusion. And almighty recent too because the moist grasses hadn't yet sprung back upright, which would happen quickly with healthy, thoroughly watered grass like this.

If Alex hadn't done it, and nobody else from town knew about this place, then it was all too possible that Longarm's nasty bowman might be the one who'd been camping at this water.

"Go back to the cart. Now."

Alex turned pale and hurried back down toward the waiting cart and horse while Longarm held his Thunderer at the ready and eased slowly forward.

Chapter 27

Longarm cursed.

The campsite was empty. Whoever it was who had stayed here was gone, and he had left nothing behind. Nothing that he would have to come back for.

He left little enough behind even in the way of sign that Longarm could read.

A small fire pit had been scooped out of the sand in the dry creekbed. It was impossible to tell how many nights the pit had been used, but Longarm knew for sure that it had been used at some time during the night just past. The ashes were still warm, their heat retained far into the day because after use the pit had been carefully covered over with sand again so as to leave no obvious sign.

Longarm could see where the man's bedroll had been spread. He found a few indistinct impressions left by the man's boots. But nothing clear enough to give him an idea of how tall the man was or how heavy.

There was nothing at all here, in fact, to tell Longarm for sure that the man who had camped by this hidden marsh was the same man with the bow who kept wanting to murder a certain deputy marshal.

The truth was that Longarm didn't need any such evidence.

He had a gut feeling as he stood beside the abandoned camp that told him this was the place where his attacker had hidden between ambush attempts.

The feeling he got here was one of being set on edge, with all his nerves atingle and all his senses sharpened.

This *was* where the bowman hid. Longarm knew it absolutely even in the absence of hard evidence to support the fact. It was simply so.

He shoved the Colt back into his holster and hurried up the bank to Alex. If the man with the bow came back while she was out of his sight...

He was being foolish, probably. There was damn small chance of that.

Still he felt better once he was beside her again.

"What is it, dear?"

He told her what he had seen and added what he suspected. "I'd appreciate it, though, if you'd keep that to yourself. I don't want word of this place to get around town."

"Oh?"

He smiled, but there was no warmth or humor at all in the expression. "Coyotes come back to the same lair over and over again."

"Oh. You're going to... waylay him here?"

"Maybe. If he comes back. It's worth a try."

"But should you try to do this yourself, dear? Shouldn't you report this to... Oh!" She clamped a hand over her mouth.

Longarm laughed, genuinely this time. "That's right, honey. I'm the guy other folks report their troubles to. I'm the one whose job it is to do something about it."

Alex threw herself against Longarm and wrapped her arms tight around him in a burst of sudden fear for his safety. "I guess I just hadn't thought, hadn't realized. How stupid of me. Oh, Longarm, now I'll be so worried about you. Every minute you aren't with me.''

He stroked her hair and gentled her with soft touching and slow kisses. "Then we'll just have to see that I spend a lot of minutes with you, won't we? To keep you from worrying any more than necessary."

She bobbed her head but still seemed worried.

He gave her a moment to calm down, then turned and guided her back to the cart. "Tell you what, honey. We'll go back to town and you can introduce me to this Mrs. Warren. We'll see if she's willing to let me ship that camera box back to the Eastman Company. If she is, I'll leave you with your daddy and carry it on down to Coldwater to the post office. The quicker the thing gets off, the quicker it'll be back and we can look at those pictures."

Alex seemed in complete agreement with that plan, and Longarm knew why. If he was in Coldwater, Texas, mailing a package, he couldn't be out here beside this marsh waiting to shoot a man. Or be shot at.

Longarm smiled to himself as he handed Alex up onto the cart seat.

That was exactly what he wanted her to be thinking so that she wouldn't worry while he was away.

No need to mention to her that tonight instead of riding straight back to Oak Creek from Coldwater he would take a little swing toward the west and sneak in on the marsh. See if the gentleman with the bow was in camp again.

He climbed onto the cart beside Alex and looked around, getting his bearings from the contours of the land so he would be able to find his way back here from the south tonight.

Chapter 28

He made it to Coldwater in time to catch the postmaster before the window was closed for the evening. Not by much, but he made it in time.

"Afternoon, neighbor. Something I can do for you?" The Coldwater postmaster, who doubled as a greengrocer and on weekends as a water witch, smiled pleasantly.

Longarm introduced himself, and the man's smile became even wider. "Heard a couple of you boys was in the vicinity. Always glad to see another civil servant. My name is Charles McRae. You can call me Mac, though. Most everybody does."

"My pleasure, Mac. And I'm Longarm to my friends."

"Longarm it is then, friend." The postmaster of Coldwater, Texas, seemed genuinely warm and welcoming. No skeletons in his closets. "How can I help you?"

"I need to mail this off quick as you can rush it there." Longarm set onto the counter the small, burlap-padded box containing Mrs. Warren's Eastman camera. The lady had agreed willingly enough to ship it to Rochester early once she understood the urgency of Longarm's need. And once Longarm explained that he would be paying for her film development and a replacement camera for her. She'd been considerably reluctant until that point of discussion was made.

Mac glanced at the address that had been written in several places on the outside of the container, following the instructions that came with the camera. "I'll get 'er there for you, Longarm, but I can't say that I'll do it very quick. Long way to York State, you know. Take, oh, two or three weeks to get there, I'd think. No way I can put a rush on it. The government goes right by the book on these things. But then an officer like you would know about that. I'm sure you have to follow the book same as I do."

"Yes, sir, I suppose I do."

"You still want to send it even though it might not be quick?"

"Reckon I don't have much choice, Mac."

McRae nodded and began plucking rubber stamps off a metal carousel behind his window, smacking them first onto an ink pad and then onto the package until the thing looked like it had been decorated by a circus clown. He used practically every stamp he had at least once, some of which, like Perishable, didn't seem to have much of anything to do with the contents of the package but went right on there anyway.

Mac looked up and winked at him. "Maybe with all this on it, it'll travel a little faster. Get somebody's attention."

Longarm smiled and thanked him for the effort. "I appreciate you trying, Mac."

"Anything for a new friend, Longarm." He weighed the now gaudy package and calculated the postage. Longarm paid for it out of his own pocket.

"You're working up there at Oak Creek, aren't you, Longarm? You and that fellow from Arkansas?" Mac asked as Longarm was about to turn away from the counter.

"That's right."

"There's a favor you might do for me then if you would."

"If I can, sure."

Mac turned toward the wall rack of letter boxes behind him and dug a thick sheaf of envelopes out of the pigeonhole labeled GENERAL DELIVERY. "Got a bunch of letters in here for folks in Oak Creek. Post Office doesn't know where to deliver 'em so they've been sending them to me here in Coldwater, though I keep telling them we don't have any delivery service up there. And not so many of those folks been coming down to pick up what I'm holding for them. It'd be a real help to me if you'd carry them along when you go back and see that they get to the addressees. I couldn't trust them to just anybody, mind, but seeing as how you're a federal employee the same as I am, I think it fits onto the pages of the book all right."

"I'd be glad to do that for you, Mac."

"Good. I do hate to see mail piling up undelivered like this." Mac tidied the letters—there must have been a dozen or more envelopes in the bunch—into a neat stack and tied a string around them to form a compact bundle. "They're in your official care now, Deputy," Mac said as he handed them through the window.

"I'll see them distributed first thing tomorrow," Longarm promised. He glanced down at the packet in his hand. The topmost letter was addressed to Merle Dyche, Main Street, Town of Oak Creek, N.M.L. (Indian Territories), U.S.A. Which seemed a long way around to tell it but which was getting the job done.

Longarm touched the brim of his Stetson to his new friend Mac and walked out to his horse. His thoughts were on supper. He would want a good meal before he headed north again, because tonight was likely to be a long one spent waiting beside the hidden marsh for his bowman to come home. He unstrapped the near pocket of his saddlebags and tucked the packet of envelopes into it.

Halfway through the task of rebuckling the saddle pocket he stopped.

Then threw his head back and roared with laughter.

Shit, why not?

Longarm chuckled softly to himself a moment more as he finished securing the bag closed, then swung onto his saddle and went looking for the best restaurant Coldwater, Texas, had to offer to a hungry traveler. With any kind of luck maybe he'd run into Ranger Vent and have some pleasant company while he ate.

Longarm's jaw shuddered and his teeth clacked together as he swallowed back a yawn that had been wanting to sneak out for the past three quarters of an hour.

It was well past midnight, and the SOB with the bow hadn't yet come in to camp.

Longarm was lying on the south side of the dry wash with his Winchester laid on the ground before him and a slight breeze drifting up his back and trying to curl in underneath his shirt collar.

There was moonlight enough that a man could see fairly well once his sight adjusted to the dark, so Longarm'd had to leave his horse picketed half a mile back from the dry creek. It wouldn't do to leave the horse where the bowman might spot it and be spooked away.

Longarm expected the bowman to come in on the north side of the wash from the direction of Oak Creek.

But so far that was just theory.

So far all he'd seen come to the greenery around the water seep was a succession of coyotes, bobcats, birds and antelope. There would have been smaller creatures coming to water in the night too, but Longarm was too far away to be able to see them.

Other creatures could find them, though. Like the predators who roamed the dark. All around him the silence of the night was interrupted periodically by the shrill, near-hysterical yip of coyotes as the small hunters announced their supper plans, and once he heard the moaning yowl of a frustrated lynx.

Longarm blinked, trying to drive the gritty feeling out of his eyes, and held his chin up high. The position put a strain on a man's neck; by morning he would be sore. But a fella who rested his head while he was trying to keep watch tended to snore while he was making his ambush. Sleep could sneak up on a man and claim him without his ever knowing it was happening until daybreak tipped the game to him.

Longarm was an old hand at waiting, though. He passed the time thinking about Alex Dyche's warm, vibrant body moving beneath his. And about the packet of letters that were buckled securely inside his saddlebags.

Just to be double safe with those letters lest the horse pull loose and wander off in the night he'd pulled the saddlebags off his cantle and hidden them close to where the horse was picketed. Postmaster McRae took them seriously, and Longarm didn't want to let him down or the folks of Oak Creek.

He thought about Alex some more, to the point where he decided he'd best quit thinking about Alex and try to concentrate on something more comfortable. Too much thought about that girl and a fella couldn't rest comfortable lying on his belly.

He tried thinking about the son of a bitch with the bow instead. That melted his hard-on quick enough.

Vigilant as Longarm was, the bowman came in damn near undetected.

He was within fifteen yards of the willow thicket before Longarm saw him. He hadn't made a sound that reached the thirty or so yards across the wash.

The SOB was good.

He came in quiet and sneaky, no sign of a horse close by, even though there was no reason he should think the marsh would be covered.

One moment there was nothing but emptiness in front of Longarm.

The next there was a dark, silent shadow moving hunched over and slow in the soft sand.

The bastard came in so slick that Longarm honestly didn't

145

know if he'd come down off the bank or had walked up the wash bottom.

It took a savvy man to get in that far without Longarm spotting him.

He was carrying something in his hand. The bow probably, though it was too dark for Longarm to see for sure. There was a bundle carried over his shoulder. His bedroll, most likely.

Longarm watched, not yet reaching for the Winchester, while the bowman spread his bedroll on the soft grass beside the willows, then lay down on it without pulling his boots off.

That wasn't good. Longarm had been hoping the bowman would build himself a fire tonight. Give Longarm a better look at him and destroy his night vision at the same time. Apparently the guy was not going to be that cooperative. Either he'd already eaten or only risked the fires for breakfast when there wouldn't be any worries about seeing in the dark. Longarm frowned.

The easy way to do this, of course, would be for Longarm to simply lie right here where he was and plant a rifle slug into the SOB's middle. Safe, secure and effective.

Unfortunately, dammit, Longarm didn't know for certain sure that this was the man who was so interested in committing murder.

He could be—likely wasn't but *could* be—any kind of bummer on the drift.

He could be a hunter who'd gotten himself lost or a cowboy whose horse broke a leg and stranded him here or . . . or practically any damn thing.

And Billy Vail kinda frowned on deputies who went around shooting civilians because they *might* be guilty of something.

For that matter, Longarm wouldn't much favor that attitude himself.

So it looked like he was going to have to do this by the book. Which was also the hard way.

Longarm rubbed his palms across the seams of his trousers, then picked up the Winchester.

He came to his knees and held the rifle aimed and ready.

"You there. You're under arrest."

Chapter 29

Shee-*it*, this son of a bitch was good.

The last words weren't out of Longarm's mouth before there was a blossom of quick flame from across the wash, and a bullet was sizzling past Longarm's left ear. No bow this time. But then no need for stealth here.

Longarm's Winchester roared and bucked, but the bastard was already moving, rolling off his bedroll and diving for the willows.

Longarm levered another round into the chamber and sent a searching shot low into the brush where the bowman had just disappeared.

There was no scream of pain. But then Longarm hadn't much expected one. Hoped for it but hadn't really expected it.

He dropped to his belly behind the rock that had sheltered him through the night hours and levered a fresh cartridge into the Winchester.

"You're wanted for questioning only," Longarm shouted. "Come out and give yourself up. I won't shoot."

The man fired again, the muzzle flash lighting up the fringe of the willow thicket.

Again the slug came uncomfortably close.

The bastard really was good. Using a handgun at night at this range, his shots should have passed within a distance that would be measured in yards, not feet or inches.

Longarm shifted his aim to the right side of the willows, figuring the guy would roll as quick as he'd fired, and triggered another round from the Winchester into the brush.

An answering shot came back at him. And from the same damned place where the man had been before. He'd figured Longarm would be expecting him to move and so had stayed right where he was, damn him.

Would he make that same assumption again? One way to find out. Longarm shot into the spot where the man had twice fired.

This time the answering fire was from just to the left of there.

Trying to nail this guy was like trying to shoot a snake that was half seen in deep grass.

"I only want to talk to you," Longarm called.

His only answer was silence.

"Give yourself up, dammit. You have no place to go, man. Give it up and you won't be hurt."

Silence.

Longarm grunted and settled down with the Winchester shoved out in front of him.

If the guy wanted to play a waiting game, that was just fine by Longarm.

Daylight would be along by-and-by. And the guy had no place to run to in the meantime. There was no cover he could use to escape from those willows without exposing himself.

Already Longarm's night vision was returning.

And he could have the patience of Job when it came to the difference between an easy arrest and a hole in his gut.

Daybreak would be quite soon enough, thank you.

He lay quiet and ready but no longer tense. He wished

for a cheroot but not so badly that he was willing to die for one, no matter what the shopworn expression to that effect claimed.

Yeah, daybreak would be just fine.

Longarm cussed and kicked a spray of fine, gritty sand into the air.

The fucker was gone.

Gone!

Impossible.

But he'd done it.

Longarm had waited until the sun was well off the horizon and the light was strong and steady before he put a sneak on the willow thicket and came up onto it from the bank overlooking the marsh, the same place he'd stood with Alex yesterday.

He'd spent a solid half hour examining every square inch of ground and foliage in sight, searching for any hint of color or texture that would indicate there was something or someone hiding down there.

He'd come up empty.

Now he'd gone through every inch of the thicket kicking and stomping, looking for a man or for so much as a rabbit hole where the SOB could've been hiding.

The thicket and the marsh were empty.

There was nobody home.

It seemed impossible, but there it was.

The man had slipped away. Somehow.

The only tiny, faint, vaguely remote possibility Longarm could think of that would have allowed such a thing would be if the guy started moving just as quick as he'd fired that last shot last night and Longarm had fired back, when both of them had their night vision disrupted by the muzzle flashes from their guns and were half blind for a second or three.

Even at that it would have taken a real craftsman at sneakiness, a master of it, to pull it off when everything around the willows was exposed to plain sight. A damned magician at it.

No damn body was that good.

Except this guy was.

The proof of it lay right here where Longarm stood completely alone in the early morning sunshine.

He shook his head and looked over the bit of booty that was all he had gained from a hard night's work.

The bow and three almighty familiar looking arrows lay on the grass beside the marsh, abandoned there when the guy jumped for the willows. The bow was a crude but effective homemade thing that had been carved out of some pale, resilient wood. Osage orange, most likely. The arrows were exactly like the mates Longarm had seen altogether too well already.

So much for any worries that the camper last night might have been an innocent bystander.

Longarm should have just shot the son of a bitch when he went to sleep.

But then hindsight is always wonderful, isn't it. Longarm grunted and reached for a cheroot. There was no reason now why he couldn't have one.

The man had also left behind his bedroll. Unfortunately it gave no information about its owner. The canvas ground cloth and bedroll cover was a dark brown commercial item that could be purchased in practically any decently stocked store west of the Big Muddy, and the blankets that it held were perfectly ordinary three-point trade blankets like you could buy anyplace where the bedrolls were sold.

The whole bedroll outfit, he noticed, looked new, barely used enough to have gotten dusty. The blankets still smelled clean and fresh and just off some store's shelf. The canvas of the bedroll cover smelled of the sizing or dye or whatever it is that new canvas smells of.

Longarm supposed that was a clue to something, but he couldn't decide what.

It sure as hell didn't mean that the bowman/gunman/SOB from last night was some pilgrim new to this country. Hardly that. Longarm couldn't think of half a dozen tough and salty hombres who could have gotten away from him last night. But this guy had. He wasn't any kind of pilgrim.

Tucked in between the blankets where it would have ridden as part of the roll when traveling there was a small cloth sack, but all it held were some twists of jerky and a fist-sized chunk of yellow cheese. There was no coffee or tea in the poke.

A grease stain discolored the side of the cloth bag. Longarm smelled that too. Bacon oils. So the man'd had a slab of bacon too and must have used that up first before he figured to start in on the more durable cheese and jerky. No wonder he hadn't started a fire last night. The foods he was carrying now didn't need cooking, and he wasn't giving himself the luxury of coffee.

That was interesting, though. Apart from telling about this guy's degree of caution—as if Longarm needed any reminders in that direction—his choice of foods meant that he wasn't counting on resupplying himself in Oak Creek.

He'd been in town often enough. Longarm knew that for certain sure after the attempts on his life and the accidental wound Alex had taken for him. But the guy wasn't planning on showing himself in any of the stores so he could buy perishable foods.

There would be a reason for that.

Was he the fake William Mann and feared he might be recognized if he showed himself up close to people in Oak Creek?

Damned well possible, that one. Maybe even probable.

For the first time since he'd come down to the marsh Longarm permitted himself a smile.

If his bowman, who was now a gunman, was the phony Billy Two, Longarm practically had the SOB where he wanted him.

Close.

And for some reason the man was worried that Deputy Long was fixing to put an end to his game.

Not worried, though, that Deputy Campbell might do the

152

same? That part still didn't fit. Why had he shot at Longarm the other night but not at Campbell?

Longarm grunted, his smile fading as he tried to think through the possibilities that would make these theories logical and rational to the man who was so very good working at night or with a bow and arrows.

There was an answer, of course. There had to be. Someplace.

The problem was that Longarm wasn't seeing it.

Wasn't giving up on it either though, dammit.

He picked up the bow, braced the tail of it on the ground and stepped down hard to bend the pliant wood past its resilience and break the crude weapon in two, broke each of the arrows as well, and then tucked the jerky and cheese back into the bedding and rolled it up so he could carry it with him. No sense in leaving the bastard with any comforts to reclaim.

Longarm took a last look around to make sure he hadn't missed anything, then shouldered the ambusher's bedroll and began hiking back to his picketed horse.

Chapter 30

Longarm was past tired. After a night of expecting death to come flying out of any shadow he felt positively frazzled. His eyes burned and his head ached, and every noise he heard sounded like it was being filtered through a tin bucket before it reached his ears.

One nice thing, though. He no longer had to worry that every man on the street might be the one who was trying to get behind Longarm's back. Longarm's boy wasn't among them.

"First a drink," he said as he approached the men who were having breakfast in Merle Dyche's place. "Then a platter of pork chops and fried 'taters about yea high." He held his hand a foot and a half off the table. "And then you and me need to do some talking, Mr. Mayor," Longarm said with a smile.

"Good news?"

"Not the news I been wanting to hear, but I think you'll be happy with it."

Merle gave him a questioning look, but Longarm refused to elaborate until his other needs had been met.

The mayor's rye hadn't gotten any better since Longarm last tasted it, but Longarm's response to it sure had. At this point he'd have been happy—well, almost—to have another shot of that rotgut Merle had set out for him and Campbell the other night.

The whiskey warmed his stomach and took some of the fur off his tongue.

Breakfast—biscuits and bacon and half a gallon of gravy—did an even better job of making him feel human. It tasted so good he didn't even mind that it wasn't what he'd ordered.

"You were saying?" Merle asked as the waiter cleared away a plate that looked clean enough that it might never have been used since its last washing.

Longarm grinned at him. He turned and picked up the saddlebags he'd draped over the back of his chair when he came in.

"Gather the folks around, Mr. Mayor. The United States mail is here. And while you're at it, you might want to have somebody find Deputy Marshal Campbell and have him come too."

Dyche clouded up and looked like he was wanting to rain all over Deputy Marshal Long.

"Trust me, Merle. Please. I'm too damn worn out to want to go through this more'n once."

Dyche hesitated for a moment. Then he smiled and nodded. "All right, Longram. Long as you know we don't like it. We aren't exactly fond of your partner."

"You will," Longarm promised with a grin. He didn't bother correcting the mayor about partnerships and who Longarm was willing to buddy up with.

He had another glass of the so-so rye, then propped his boots on the edge of the chair Merle had just vacated and lighted a cheroot to enjoy while he waited.

Merle had most of the men of Oak Creek assembled in

the big saloon room within ten minutes. It took a little longer for Campbell to get there.

Longarm grunted and sat upright. He unbuckled his saddlebag pocket and pulled out the sheaf of letters Mac McRae had given him, snapped the string and tossed it aside.

"Mr. Mayor, I believe this here letter is addressed to you. Take a look at it, please, and tell me if that's so."

Merle frowned, puzzled, but he stepped forward and accepted the envelope Longarm handed him. He glanced down at it, shrugged and said, "It's mine, sure."

Longarm chuckled and said. "Read off exactly what it says on there so you know it's your letter. Out loud, please."

"Longarm!"

"Just do it, Merle. Please."

The mayor of Oak Creek shrugged again and did as Longarm asked, reading the address and return address aloud so everyone in the place could hear.

"It's from Cousin Byron," Monroe said to somebody, his tone of voice suggesting that he was just as confused about this as his brother was.

Longarm picked up the next letter. "This one is to a fella name of Albert Kronsky. Is he here?"

"Here," a short, middle-aged man with muttonchop whiskers said. He came forward and accepted the letter. "Do you want me to read too?"

"Please, Mr. Kronsky."

The gentleman had to take a pair of spectacles out of his coat pocket and put them on, then did as he was asked.

"Longarm, what the hell is—"

"Humor me, fellas."

He worked through the entire stack that way until all fourteen letters had been publicly delivered. They all had to wait until one man who hadn't come to the saloon was fetched from his home. Someone said with a snicker that he'd still been abed, although he didn't look sick when he was finally dragged in to receive his mail from home. He looked somewhat pissed off but not at all sick. Just married, maybe but not ailing.

"Is that it? Can we go now that you've finished playing?" Kronsky asked when the last letter had been handed out and the last addresses read off.

Longarm grinned and motioned toward Deputy Campbell. "You listen up to this too, Lew. Now we've all witnessed what just happened here. And personally, I don't know that it will have any effect on what some court of law will rule when the time comes.

"But my point is, an officially appointed agent of the United States government, namely Postmaster Charles 'Mac' McRae in Coldwater, Texas, asked me, as an officially appointed agent of the United States government, namely being a United States deputy marshal, to protect and to deliver those letters to their rightful addressees. Namely you, Mr. Mayor, and you and you and . . . I think you get the picture."

At least a few of the men were starting to get the rest of the picture too. Longarm could see it in the smiles that were beginning to spread over their faces.

"What this implies, gentlemen, though without a test case in a federal court, is that the government of these United States has now officially recognized the town of Oak Creek as existing. And I would kinda think that that state of affairs has to be accepted by other officers, officials, authorities or whatever representing the government until or unless some official agency, like the court for instance, rules otherwise."

Longarm gave Merle Dyche a wink and Deputy Campbell a grin.

"Bullshit," Campbell blurted.

"That's your opinion, Lew. And you are entitled to it, just like I'm entitled to mine. What you and me both know, though, is that it's the job of the courts to look at opinions and decide what is fact. So I suggest you and me both leave these folks be until some court gets around to doing that."

"These people are here illegally," Campbell insisted.

"Hell, Lew, they were here illegal, sure. But that's my point. This business of the government you and me both work for recognizing the town, that changes everything.

Makes it seem to me that they must be here legal unless the government changes its mind later on. For right now, though, the government says there's a town here. Recognizes that strong enough to deliver mail here. So you and me got no kick with these people till a judge tells us different."

"You're bending—"

"No, sir. I'm just going by the book. Going by what the government itself says is so. Surely you don't figure to argue with the government, Lew. Why, you and me are sworn to uphold the law, not to look for some way around it." He winked at Merle again, and the men in the place began to laugh.

Campbell got red faced but didn't say anything. The little deputy from Fort Smith turned and stalked away.

"Why, Longarm, I think you've gone and ruined his whole day," Kronsky said.

"Just going by the book, fellas," he said.

"We surely do thank you, Longarm," Monroe and Merle both said almost at the same time.

"If you want to pass thanks around, give them to Amos Vent. He's the one who had the idea first. Remember how embarrassed you were that day I met you and you didn't know who I was yet? You spilled Amos's beans then. Then yesterday when Mac gave me these letters to carry up here for him, well, I happened to think about that and figured it might be twisted just enough to get Campbell off your backs. One thing you'd best keep in mind, though. Your legal status here is still in question. You'd best work real hard at getting a postmaster appointed here and whatever else you can think of that supports your claims. Don't think this ends anything. It just gives you room to breathe while you work the rest of it out for yourselves."

His warning did nothing to dampen the high spirits of the men of Oak Creek, though.

Didn't do much to stop them from wanting to buy him drinks either.

It was really a shame that Longarm was still feeling so

tired, because he could have had himself a hell of a party if he'd stayed. And all on the other fellow's dime too.

As it was he excused himself as soon as he decently could and headed for the room that he hadn't been able to enjoy in much too long.

He needed to get a few hours' sleep and then do some thinking about the entirely too slippery son of a bitch who might, or might not, be the fake Billy Two.

Chapter 31

Longarm woke with a start, the Colt in his hand and finger on the trigger.

"Don't shoot!" The whisper was frightened. And very high pitched.

Longarm blinked the sleep out of his eyes and hurriedly stuffed the revolver back into the holster that was hanging on the bedpost.

"You shouldn't be here, Alex. Your father and uncle aren't thirty feet away."

"I came in the back way, dear. No one saw me. And no one will bother you while they think you're sleeping. You're our town hero, you know."

Longarm didn't much feel like anybody's hero. He might have held things off a little while as far as the people of Oak Creek and their problems were concerned, but he hadn't done a damn thing yet to help Billy Vail's friend Billy Two.

"What are you doing here?" he whispered.

Alex tiptoed forward. The light in the room was dim from the shade that had been drawn over the only window, but there was plenty enough light for him to see what she was doing.

She laid her bonnet down on the tiny bureau that was the only furniture in the hotel room except for the lumpy bed, then turned and smiled at him. She gave her head a toss, sending her unpinned chestnut hair cascading over her shoulders and onto the front of her duster.

"Oh," he said, and smiled back at her.

It felt like he'd had four or five hours of sleep since he left the men in the bar. Under the circumstances that seemed like plenty.

Alex unbuttoned the duster she always wore in public and let it fall onto the floor. Her dress followed quickly, and she stepped out of her shoes. She was not wearing stockings or a chemise under the street garments.

This time, he was pleased to see, there wasn't any shyness about her. No lingering fears that he would think she was ugly or that he wouldn't want her.

This time she was able to stand naked and proud in front of him, able to forget the burn scars on her body quite as easily as he did.

And except for those, her body was fine indeed. Slim and straight and nicely formed.

She came to him and bent, cupping her breasts in her palms and offering them to his lips, first one and then the other.

He suckled on her, and Alex moaned.

She crouched on the bed over him, and his hand slid between her slender thighs to find the soft patch of hair there and play with the tiny, pink button of her pleasure.

"If you don't quit groaning so loud the whole barroom's gonna hear," he whispered.

Alex giggled. "I'll try to be good."

"Good, hell, you're great. What I want you to be is quiet."

She laughed and pulled the sheet off his body.

Longarm hadn't completely stripped when he lay down for his daytime sleep. Alex made a face and impatiently helped him out of his balbriggans. "Why do these things have to be so awkward," she complained.

"If you'd sent a boy over to warn me you were coming I could've gotten ready."

She stuck her tongue out at him, then laughed.

"Shhh."

"Sorry." Not that she looked or acted particularly sorry.

She snuggled down against him with a sigh, her mouth covering his and her hands every bit as busy now as his were.

"I got to say," he whispered, "once you get the idea for something you do learn just fine."

That pleased her too. She giggled, masking the sound of it by pressing her lips tight against his, then turned and wiggled around so they were lying head to foot.

Yeah, the girl did learn things *just* fine.

"I dunno," Longarm whispered. "This time I might be the one doing the hollering."

"Shhh."

"Yes, ma'am"

She smelled of soap and rosewater, and her satin-soft skin was slightly damp. She must have just stepped out of a tub before she sneaked across the street to him. Clean is always a woman's most enjoyable scent, just like fat is always a horse's prettiest color.

Longarm nuzzled and nipped at her, and Alex groaned and opened herself to him. Her vee was wet, but it wasn't with soap or water.

She was every bit as busy as he was. Longarm had taught her the basics, but Alex was doing just dandy with the refinements all on her own. She was an inventive little thing.

"Quit slurping so loud," he told her, and she laughed.

"One other thing I'd best warn you about," he whispered. "You keep that up, and you're gonna get a mouthful."

"I already have a mouthful, thank you, and I'm enjoying it thoroughly."

"That ain't the kind I meant."

"I know. But you promised. Remember? You said I could."

"Dang. Try and be polite and look what happens."

She giggled and bent to him again with renewed effort. Faster now. Deeper.

Longarm groaned and tried to hold the pleasure back as long as he possibly could so he could prolong the additional pleasure of getting there.

There was only so much a man could do about that, though.

Long before Longarm was willing, Alex drew him out of himself and into her.

He shuddered and spasmed, his back rigid and his muscles straining as the hot fluids pumped in one hard jet after another like they would go on forever.

Alex stayed with him, her hands cupping his balls and her tongue ever busy until the last drop had been released and Longarm fell back limp against the now sweaty sheets.

"Thank you," she said. She smiled up at him.

"*You* are thanking *me*?"

"Mm-hmm."

"I knew there was something about you that I liked almighty well," he said with a grin.

She picked his flaccid shaft up on the ends of her fingers and examined it closely for a moment, then bent her head to lick up a final drop of milky white semen. She gave him a kittenish smile and then kissed the damp head of it with a sigh.

"That was nice," she said.

"Was, hell," he corrected. "We've hardly started. Unless you're in a hurry to get somewhere."

"Really?"

"You don't sound too awful unhappy about it, so yeah. Really."

Alex laughed and turned, throwing herself onto his chest and pressing herself tight against him. She sighed again. "I never knew it was possible to be this happy, Longarm. I certainly never thought that . . . you know . . . that I would be."

He stroked her hair and her lovely, unblemished back. "I can't think of anybody I'd rather see happy than you, Alex." He meant that, too.

"Oh, my."

"What?"

"This." She touched him. "I love the way it feels when it's growing like that. You're all ready again."

"Said I would be, didn't I?"

She smiled and gave him a squeeze. "Do you want me to . . . you know . . . again?"

He shook his head. "Not this time, pretty girl." He rolled her onto her back and fondled her.

"Mmm, this is nice too, dear," she said. She reached for him. "But now I'm all confused. I don't know what I like the best."

"Tell you what. We'll try everything." He laughed. "And if you still can't decide, why we'll just start over. Tell me when you have it worked out."

Alex clutched him to her with a fierce and unexpected intensity as Longarm's lean, hard body fused into hers.

Chapter 32

Longarm waited until dark, then excused himself from the crowd of men who were still celebrating—foolishly, he thought; their war was far from being won even if a battle had been gained—inside the saloon.

There was no sign of Deputy Campbell. Someone said they'd seen him packing his gear and riding out toward the north, the direction the fake Billy Two had taken when he fled Oak Creek several weeks earlier. The townsman said Campbell was acting like he had no intention of returning. That was just fine by Custis Long. It was bad enough having enemies hiding in the bushes. But at least a man could defend himself freely if he knew all the ambushers were enemies. Having allies, even unpleasant ones like Lew Campbell, lurking in the brush complicated matters; he couldn't shoot at the first twig snap if it might be another officer he was throwing down on.

He left his horse tied conspicuously on the street where he'd left it earlier and made his way on foot through the shadows. Searching. Hunting for the quick and able gunman who wanted to kill him.

The ambush at the man's camp last night had failed. That didn't mean Longarm was willing to quit.

The fake Billy Two was here, in Oak Creek, and Longarm wanted him. It would be the only truly effective way to clear Billy Vail's old friend and get the judge in Fort Smith to call back his warrants.

With any kind of luck—and the man had to have balls cast in solid brass to've been able to accomplish his sneaks in the middle of town for so long already—the gunman would still be here, would still be wanting to put a bullet into Deputy Long.

Longarm, in fact, was counting on it.

He stuck to the alleys, investigated the sheds, very nearly slaughtered two cats and a half-grown pup when they surprised him in the dark.

There was . . . not a damn thing.

Nothing, at any rate, that was of any official interest. His alley snooping disclosed that one of the local wives was having a back-porch affair with her neighbor's teenage son, and that another family had a daughter of only eleven or twelve who was a prodigy at piano playing, classical stuff that wasn't especially to Longarm's taste but that was nonetheless damned well played. Also that another gentleman of high local repute had holes in his longjohns; the family wash was still hanging on the line, which was just as well since seeing the clothes left out overnight kept Longarm from walking throat-high into the clothesline.

He figured he could have lived quite happily without any of that knowledge.

What he wanted, of course, was a sniff of the damned gunman.

He found nothing.

He made four trips through the small town, investigating every shadow, peering behind every barrel and into every shed. It was like the gunman had taken the night off.

Or given up and ridden away?

Longarm wasn't proud. He'd have been pleased for Campbell to get the collar if the two of them, the Fort Smith deputy and the fugitive who was using William Mann's name, blundered into each other somewhere out on the high plains.

But . . .

If the bastard wasn't in Oak Creek, maybe he was hiding somewhere close by, waiting until he thought the timing was better so he could sneak in and have another crack at his target.

Longarm quit the alleys and slipped away from the lights and low noises of town, into the dry, ugly country around the struggling little community.

He found three likely places where a man might want to hide himself and observe the comings and goings in Oak Creek. All three of them showed traces, scuffed footprints and crushed grasses, that indicated someone indeed had been there. But on other nights. There was no one hiding in any of them now. The only signs of life he found on his nocturnal ramble were those of coyotes and jackrabbits and the occasional packrat.

Somewhere around one in the morning Longarm cursed and went back to his hotel room.

If he couldn't find the gunman, well, maybe the son of a bitch would be obliging enough to come to him once more.

As a final precaution he made one more circuit through the town alleys, then deliberately showed himself on the street as he went back to the hotel and showed lamplight in his room window.

He waited about long enough that he could have stripped and washed up a bit before hitting the sack, then blew the lamp out and retired not to the bed but to a corner of the small room where he could wait wide awake and alert with his Colt ready to hand. His nap—so nicely interrupted earlier—left him comfortable enough that he could make it through the night now without sleeping.

He reassured himself once more that the Thunderer was loose in his holster, then crossed his arms and began another patient vigil in the hope that he would be able to trap the ambusher and turn the game on him.

Chapter 33

Longarm stabbed a bite of pork chop like he was wanting to punish the fried meat and frowned as he bit into it. He had spent a sleepless night for nothing. He hadn't found the gunman, and the damn gunman hadn't found him.

But the man *had* to still be here. Had to be. Dammit.

He chewed and swallowed mechanically, scarcely aware of what he was eating, and followed it with a draught of hot coffee.

Damn it all anyhow.

Tonight maybe he could...

"Longarm?"

He looked up, still frowning.

"Look, if I'm disturbing something here..."

The frown evaporated and became a smile of welcome instead. "No, Monroe. My fault. I was just fretting about something. You ain't bothering me. Glad for the company, in fact. Sit down. Let me buy you some breakfast."

"I've already eaten, thanks. I just stopped by to give you

a message." The shopkeeper smiled. "Though I don't know what put the bee in Alexandra's bonnet so."

"Oh?"

"The child was up half the night last night," her father said. "Working out in that studio of hers. Can you believe it? At night? She never tries to work at night. That's why I built all that glass in for her, so she'd have natural light to work by. Then last night she up and hauls out every lamp we own and half the lamps and lanterns off my store shelves so she can work while it's dark out. How do I figure that one?"

Longarm gave the man a sympathetic grin. Alex was one fine girl, but hell, every man knows that every woman is beyond comprehension. Alex Dyche was no exception to the rule.

Longarm already knew, of course, that Alex had been working in her studio last night. He'd seen her every time he made his way through the alleys and hidden corners. He just hadn't particularly thought it so unusual for someone to be painting after dark.

"Anyway," Monroe said, "she asked me to ask you to come see her this morning. Says she has something for you."

"For me?" Longarm was flattered. The painting Alex worked on last night must have been intended for him. He was glad now that her easel had been turned away from the windows. If she'd been making a surprise for him he wouldn't have wanted it given away by his snooping.

"Uh-huh. Didn't tell me what it was, though." Monroe acted about half piqued that his daughter hadn't confided the secret to him.

Longarm glanced down at his partially eaten breakfast. Between his earlier mood and his present curiosity he wasn't really hungry anyway. He pushed the plate away and drained off the last of his coffee. "Reckon I better go see what she's up to, Monroe."

"Oh, I doubt it's all that important."

"Aw, I was done anyhow. Too fretful to be hungry.

Besides, now you got me to wondering about that daughter of yours. Let's go see what she's done." It occurred to him after he said it that the invitation for Monroe to come along might not've been such a good idea. Like if Alex had painted a picture of herself naked or something. Then he reconsidered. She wouldn't have done a thing like that, and then sent the message by her father, no sir. He stood and dropped his napkin on the table. Monroe led the way across the street to his store and on through the building to Alex's glass-walled studio.

"Good morning, Marshal Long." Alex's words were proper enough, but there was a sparkle in her pale eyes that Longarm hoped her dad couldn't see. Or at least couldn't recognize.

"Morning, Miss Dyche."

"Daddy told you what I've been up to, I suppose."

"Nope. Just that you wanted to see me."

"It was really his idea," she said.

"It was?" Monroe exclaimed. "Now what idea of mine is this that we're talking about?"

"You remember. At supper last night when we were talking about Marshal Long needing a picture of Mr. Mann and you said—"

"That? I never thought you'd do it, honey."

"Well, I did."

"Good for you." Monroe seemed truly pleased. "Why, good for you, darling."

"You two wouldn't mind filling me in on the secret, would you?" Longarm asked.

Monroe laughed. "Not at all. It's just that for years I've been trying to convince Alex to try her hand at portraiture. She always claims she can't get the ears right. She's such a perfectionist." He sighed, but proudly. "You probably noticed in her other paintings that she never includes human figures in them. And rarely animals. Well, last night I suggested she paint a portrait of Mr. Mann. From memory, of course. But still—"

"And did you?" Longarm asked Alex.

She gave him one of the shy looks that he remembered so well, but this time it had nothing to do with shyness about her body. This time she was feeling timid about how her work would be accepted. And perhaps in the long run that was even more important than how her body might be accepted.

Almost reluctantly, she nodded. "It's over here." Her voice was very small and filled with nervousness.

She gestured toward the easel where she had been busy late into the night. It held a cloth-draped canvas.

"Can I see?" Longarm asked.

The girl sighed, and nodded again.

He wanted to give her a kiss of encouragement but couldn't with her father standing there looking on. He settled for a wink that Monroe couldn't see and gestured a brief thumbs-up as he went over to the easel and lifted the protective cloth off of it.

"Careful," Monroe said. "The paints won't have dried yet."

"Daddy!"

"Well," Monroe said defensively. "It's your first real portrait. I don't want it ruined."

Alex seemed pleased by her father's proud, supportive attitude even if she acted like she was exasperated by him.

Longarm's interest, though, was on the waist-up portrait Alex had worked so hard to paint.

He frowned and said, "The ears look fine to me, Miss Dyche. Just fine. Why, I think I'd recognize this fella anyplace now that I've seen him."

"Do you really?"

"Ayuh, I say I would. And I thank you for going to all the trouble."

"I'm really not happy with those ears. Or his nose either. I don't think I got it quite right."

"You did fine," Longarm said.

"Huh. It's perfect," her father declared. "That's him, all right. That's William Mann, right down to his watch fob. Just the way he looked when he was here stealing from us. It's a perfect likeness, honey." Monroe gave Alex a hearty kiss on the forehead. Longarm wished like hell that he was free to give her a kiss too. Except not on the forehead. And not with her father standing in the same room watching.

"You've been a big help, Miss Dyche. I mean that. A bigger help than you know."

"Really?" She sounded pleased now. And probably relieved as well now that her first attempt at portraiture was proving to be a success.

"I'll have to tell you how much of a help sometime when I have more time to talk about it." Longarm hoped Alex got the message. He was going to have to be pulling out of Oak Creek now. Yet with Monroe standing there he couldn't make her any promises or offer any hopes that he would be seeing her again, much as he would like to in the future. He shook hands with Monroe but didn't dare even that much with Alex.

"You're leaving?" she asked.

"Got to," he said. "Got some work to finish."

"Do you . . . want to take the portrait with you?"

He smiled. "Let the oils dry. I'll . . . come back for it. If that's all right with you."

The brightness returned to her eyes, and her smile told him just how all right that was with her. She nodded. "It will be here for you. Marshal Long."

"I'll count on that. Miss Dyche." The unspoken messages completed, Longarm turned and hurried off toward Merle's hotel.

He knew exactly where he was going now. And exactly what he was going to have to do once he got there, difficult though it would be.

Chapter 34

Longarm was patently obvious about what he was doing.

He tied his horse in front of the hotel on the sunny main street where anyone and everyone could see, then made separate slow trips inside to bring out his saddle, back again for his scabbarded Winchester and saddlebags, back inside again for his carpetbag to secure behind the cantle.

He wanted it clearly understood by anyone who cared to look that he was packing up and leaving.

In particular he wanted it noticed by anyone who might be laying out on the bluffs somewhere, say with a spy glass or pair of powerful field glasses.

He took his time about it and collected handshakes and gratitude from a hefty percentage of the town's population while he was going about it.

If the gunman was out there, Longarm wanted the man to see.

If the SOB wanted to try and slip ahead of Longarm's route and lay an ambush, well, that would be just fine.

Smoke the bastard out into the open and get this done with.

And if that didn't work, well, there were alternatives.

Longarm said his good-byes and tried to leave a government payment voucher with Merle Dyche for the costs of his room and meals. The Oak Creek mayor would have none of it. "It's been our pleasure, Longarm. Believe me. As much as you've done for us here, why, I'd be the worst kind of ingrate if I took your money."

"It ain't my money," Longarm pointed out. "And anyhow, remember what I told you. You only got a delay about things, not a victory. You keep after the post office, start writing letters to senators and congressmen, everything you can think of. You got a long way to go before anybody settles on the questions of land title here."

"I know," Merle said. "But I still won't take that voucher."

Longarm smiled and shook the mayor's hand warmly. They were good folks here. Tough, stubborn, determined, honest folks of the kind that many westerners don't want to admit come out of the East but so often do. He wished them well with their dreams for the future and was glad he'd been able to give them what little hope and help he had.

"Good luck to you, Merle."

"And to you, Longarm. You come back here any time. You're always welcome in this town."

Longarm touched the brim of his hat to Merle and to the other men who had gathered to see him off, then climbed onto his saddle and pointed the horse south toward Coldwater.

If he'd been trying to get away without the gunman getting ahead of him he would have chosen another route.

But that wasn't at all what he had in mind now.

"There's two ways you can get back to the railroad," Amos Vent told him over the supper table at Mrs. Cates's boarding house. "Two scheduled runs heading west tomorrow. The first to leave would be Carl Packer's freight wagon. He'll pull out at first light, but he'll be traveling slow and heavy. Won't get to Lamy and the rails for several days. Or you can wait just a few hours, see, and take the coach to Santa Rosa. It leaves just 'fore noon but moves faster. You can transfer at Santa Rosa, take another fast coach to Lamy an' reach the tracks well ahead of Carl. By a good day at the least. Longer if one of Carl's old wagons breaks down along the way."

"But you say the freight run leaves earlier?"

"That's right."

Longarm smiled. Slow and predictable. It sounded like it was made to order for what he had in mind. "Where can I find Carl Packer, Amos? I'll want to tell him that he's got a passenger for tomorrow's trip."

The Ranger raised an eyebrow but offered no objections. He had explained the situation fairly and had enough respect for Longarm to realize the tall deputy would have a reason for doing things his own way.

"We'll find him after supper, Longarm." The Ranger brightened. "If I know Carl he'll be in the saloon having himself one last go at bucking the faro table 'fore he leaves. He's a man as always loses, but that don't keep him from trying his best. An' after our obligations are met, why, I don't see no reason why you and me can't have us a farewell fling too. See if we can't take Carl's example and enjoy losing some pay." He winked. "Or whatever else seems a good idea at the time."

Longarm smiled. "Sounds all right to me, Amos."

Chapter 35

Longarm scowled.

Where in hell was that son-of-a-bitch gunman?

For four days now, Longarm had been busy making a target of himself, hoping with every passing second and every passing clump of brush or rock to hide behind that the bastard would show himself and get this business ended.

Yet there'd been nothing.

No attack. No bullet out of the distance. No gleam of sunlight off a field glass lens or a rifle barrel. Nothing.

It was becoming positively unnerving, waiting for that second shoe to drop, dammit.

Longarm scowled again and shifted position on the grubby, soot-grimed seat of the Denver & Rio Grande passenger coach. It was getting so that he wouldn't even turn his back on the rear end of the railroad car lest the gunman be trying to sneak up on him from that direction. Instead he was seated sideways on the hard bench seat with his back to the window. When they pulled out of Palmer Lake, the last stop before Denver, Longarm had scared some poor citizen half out of his mind when the guy tried to take the vacant side of Longarm's seat and like to got his head bit off.

No, Longarm wasn't in an especially good frame of mind from all this waiting and wondering when the guy would jump.

And he *had* to make his move.

Damn quick, too.

Had to put Deputy Marshal Custis Long down.

And just as important to the gunman's way of thinking, by damn, had to leave Deputy Marshal Lew Campbell alive and working at finding William Mann with those warrants for murder and fraud, at least until Longarm had been disposed of and the rest of his coldly calculated plan implemented.

Longarm had had four days to think that through, and he believed he had it figured now.

It made sense, all right, although in a twisted kind of way.

Made sense, anyhow, to that son of a bitch with the bow and the quick gun and the awful smooth style when putting on a sneak.

Jeez, this bastard was good.

Longarm wasn't afraid of any man. But he'd developed plenty of respect for this one's abilities.

Longarm grimaced and fished inside his coat for a cheroot. Only two left. It was a good thing he would be getting back to Denver so he could replenish his supply.

He pulled out the next to last smoke, bit the twist off the tip of it and spat the fleck of dark tobacco onto the floor of the rail car, then struck a match and lit up. The flavor of the cheroot was pleasant and comforting.

Where the fuck was the gunman?

The wheels of the D&RG coach clacked and jolted rhythmically over the joints in the rails below. And every clack, every jolt put them that much closer to the depot in Denver.

The man simply had to make his move. Soon. He couldn't delay much longer or his whole game would fall apart.

So where the hell was he?

Longarm gnawed at the butt of his cheroot, turning the tobacco soft and wet.

Damn the man.

Where *was* he?

Longarm stepped down off the steel step of the railroad car onto the Denver platform. Bits of dark cinder crunched underfoot, and the air smelled of coal smoke and spent steam. It was something like what Hell must smell like.

He was carrying his gear and trying to juggle it all in one hand so his right hand would be free to grab for the Colt if this was where the gunman would finally make his move.

Trying not to be obvious about it, Longarm was intent on keeping his back to the railroad coach he'd just exited while he surveyed the crowd waiting to greet people off the train.

"What the . . . ?"

He saw a familiar face. But damn sure not the one he'd been expecting. Damn sure not the one he'd last seen painted onto a canvas back at Alex Dyche's little studio.

"Billy? What the hell are you doing here?"

U.S. Marshal Billy Vail, his expression serious, pushed his way through the people on the platform to reach Longarm's side.

"We got a wire from Deputy Campbell, Longarm. Mostly he was complaining about you mixing into his case in No-Man's-Land. He also mentioned that you'd left there and were heading back this way. He's filing a formal complaint with the attorney general."

"And that's enough to bring you down here waiting to grab me off the damn train?"

Vail gave his best deputy a smile that was tinged with a deep sadness. He sighed. "You know it isn't."

"Well then?"

Vail's chest heaved again. Reluctantly, staring off into

the distance so that he didn't have to look Longarm in the eyes, he said, "I can be a stupid son of a bitch sometimes, can't I?"

"Shit, Billy, I'm sorry. You figured it out then?"

The marshal nodded. "I think so. Not all of it probably. Enough."

"How?"

"I stopped by your rooming house the other day to have a talk with Billy Two."

"Oh," Longarm said, understanding completely. "For whatever it's worth, Billy, I'm almighty sorry."

Vail nodded. The color had drained from his normally pink cheeks. He looked gray. And years older than he had the last Longarm saw him. "I . . ." he started to say. Then his jaw clamped firmly shut, and a hard look froze his face. His eyes, which had been distant and unfocused, fairly leaped with fire now.

Longarm looked in the direction where Billy was suddenly staring. He bent to set his gear down.

"No!" Vail snapped.

"Dammit, Billy, I—"

"*No*, I said." His voice was low and controlled. And sharper than Longarm had ever heard it until this moment. "He's mine," Billy Vail hissed.

"Jesus, Billy, you can't . . ."

The marshal was paying no attention to Longarm now. The deputy might not have existed for all Vail knew or cared right now.

He pulled the left side of his never-buttoned coat back out of the way.

"Billy."

Vail acted like he hadn't heard.

"Shit," Longarm complained to the empty air on the platform.

The crowd, thank goodness, was thinning. Not so many innocent bystanders around now. Longarm was glad of that.

One of the few who did remain was no bystander waiting to greet someone off the D&RG northbound.

The man was disguised. Longarm could see it now. Without Billy Vail to make the identification for him, though, he might not have seen through the false whiskers and the shabby workman's clothing. As it was, the disguise seemed pathetically obvious.

The guy had gotten ahead of him after all. Had waited for Longarm here on the platform in Denver. Of course. That would have been a perfect sort of icing on the cake of deception he was trying to put together.

And on the mindless, insulting fury he'd been trying to build inside Billy Vail's thoughts.

The bastard was as clever in his thinking as he was in the field.

"He's good, Billy. Awful good."

A tight half smile thinned the marshal's lips. "I'm better, by God. Why do you think I was the one called Billy One?"

Twenty feet away William Mann, Billy Two, Billy Vail's great and good and true old friend, saw that his last card had been played. Saw that his deception had fallen apart. His appeal to old friendship and trust was no longer working. He tugged on the hem of the ragged jacket he was wearing. The telltale bulge of the shoulder holster was there. Just like the one that matched it under Billy Vail's coat.

Longarm wanted to tell Billy that it was his place to make the arrest, dammit it. That Billy was out of practice. That Billy hadn't been in the field in much too long to be the one facing down Billy Two now.

He didn't want to distract his boss now, though.

If Longarm spoke it might be just the distracting edge that Mann needed. Longarm swallowed and forced himself to remain statue still. The slightest movement from him now might set Mann off and give him an edge on Billy One.

The son of a bitch, Longarm thought.

Mann waited until the last of the bystanders had cleared the platform, then smiled at his old and dear pal.

"I didn't expect to see you here, One."

"I did expect to see you, Two," Billy Vail said.

"You figured it out? I'll be damned."

"You never spent one night in Longarm's room, Two. I went by to talk to you. The landlady knew nothing about you. Said she hadn't seen you after that first day. I asked a few questions. The butcherboy who sells sandwiches on the Denver and Rio Grande coaches remembered you, Two. You followed Longarm south, didn't you? You were going to kill him. Going to murder one of my deputies so I would be so mad I would never give up looking for the man you claimed was an impostor. And I would think all the while that you couldn't have done it. That you'd been here in Denver when Longarm was murdered. You would have murdered Longarm and made me your alibi."

Mann shrugged. And smiled. "It could have worked, One."

"I won't argue that point with you, Two. The fact is, it didn't work. Now I am placing you under arrest on charges of murder, fraud and assault on a federal officer. Turn around, please, and put your hands on top of your head. I believe you know the procedure."

Mann chuckled. "I won't give myself up, One. Not even to you."

"Yes, Billy. Yes, you will," Billy Vail said with simple conviction. "Yes, you must."

"Aw, Billy. Surely you understand. All those years we put in. I came out of it with nothing, Billy. Not like you with your cushy marshal's appointment. I was left with nothing except some fancy crap to hang on my walls. And too little wherewithal to buy any walls. No money, no hopes, nothing. I was just trying to make myself a little stake. No harm done. It wasn't like the government needed all that useless land out there. And those rich shits from back East, there wasn't any harm done to them. It was just a little inconvenience."

"Murder is more than an inconvenience, Two, no matter who it is who's murdered."

"I can explain that, Billy. Hear me out. All I want is a few minutes. Just listen to what I have to say and—"

Mann's hand flashed with a magician's speed. A nickel-plated bulldog revolver appeared in his fist in an eyeblink.

Two revolvers roared in almost the same instant, filling the distance between the two Billys with flame and smoke.

Billy Mann blinked, a look of stark, sudden, overwhelming surprise coming into his eyes.

He stood there on the Denver & Rio Grande platform and stared down at his revolver as if accusing it.

Then his knees buckled and he pitched face forward onto the planks, the cold, unfired gun dropping out of suddenly nerveless fingers.

"I thought I told you to stay out of this, Longarm," Billy Vail said softly.

"Yeah," Longarm agreed. "So you did." He turned the big Colt Thunderer over and shucked the empty cartridge casing out onto the platform so he could replace it with a fresh round.

Beside him Billy Vail was doing the same thing with his own gun.

"It was my shot that killed him, Billy," Longarm said.

Whether that was true or not—and neither of them would ever know for sure—he hoped Billy Vail, the only Billy now, would choose to believe it. Better that than think he'd killed his old friend.

"Christ, Billy. I'm sorry."

Vail nodded, his expression coldly impassive. "I know, Longarm. But he wouldn't have expected anything different. Not really." He sighed heavily, sadly. "He was a good officer once. A good partner. I know you must find that hard to believe, but . . ." Vail's face twisted in anguish, and he couldn't speak anymore.

The two of them moved forward, toward the body, as frightened, wide-eyed faces began to appear at the door to the Denver & Rio Grande waiting room and to show themselves at the windows of the passenger coach behind them.

Watch for

LONGARM AND THE VIGILANTES

140th novel in the bold LONGARM series
from Jove

Coming in August!

A special offer for people who enjoy reading the best Westerns published today. If you enjoyed this book, subscribe now and get...

TWO FREE

A $5.90 VALUE—NO OBLIGATION

If you enjoyed this book and would like to read more of the very best Westerns being published today, you'll want to subscribe to True Value's Western Home Subscription Service. If you enjoyed the book you just read and want more of the most exciting, adventurous, action packed Westerns, subscribe now.

Each month the editors of True Value will select the 6 very best Westerns from America's leading publishers for special readers like you. You'll be able to preview these new titles as soon as they are published, FREE for ten days with no obligation.

TWO FREE BOOKS

When you subscribe, we'll send you your first month's shipment of the newest and best 6 Westerns for you to preview. With your first shipment, two of these books will be yours as our introductory gift to you absolutely FREE, regardless of what you decide to do. If you like them, as much as we think you will, keep all six books but pay for just 4 at the low subscriber rate of just $2.45 each. If you decide to return them, keep 2 of the titles as our gift. No obligation.

Special Subscriber Savings

When you become a True Value subscriber you'll save money several ways. First, all regular monthly selections will be billed at the low subscriber price of just $2.45 each. That's

WESTERNS!

at least a savings of $3.00 each month below the publishers price. Second, there is never any shipping, handling or other hidden charges—Free home delivery. What's more there is no minimum number of books you must buy, you may return any selection for full credit and you can cancel your subscription at any time. A TRUE VALUE!

Mail the coupon below

To start your subscription and receive 2 FREE WESTERNS, fill out the coupon below and mail it today. We'll send your first shipment which includes 2 FREE BOOKS as soon as we receive it.

Mail To:
True Value Home Subscription Services, Inc.
P.O. Box 5235
120 Brighton Road
Clifton, New Jersey 07015-5235

10352

YES! I want to start receiving the very best Westerns being published today. Send me my first shipment of 6 Westerns for me to preview FREE for 10 days. If I decide to keep them, I'll pay for just 4 of the books at the low subscriber price of $2.45 each; a total of $9.80 (a $17.70 value). Then each month I'll receive the 6 newest and best Westerns to preview Free for 10 days. If I'm not satisfied I may return them within 10 days and owe nothing. Otherwise I'll be billed at the special low subscriber rate of $2.45 each; a total of $14.70 (at least a $17.70 value) and save $3.00 off the publishers price. There are never any shipping, handling or other hidden charges. I understand I am under no obligation to purchase any number of books and I can cancel my subscription at any time, no questions asked. In any case the 2 FREE books are mine to keep.

Name _____

Address _____ Apt. # _____

City _____ State _____ Zip _____

Telephone # _____

Signature _____

(if under 18 parent or guardian must sign)
Terms and prices subject to change.
Orders subject to acceptance by True Value Home Subscription Services, Inc.

LONGARM

Explore the exciting Old West with one of the men who made it wild!

__LONGARM AND THE BLOOD BOUNTY #116	0-515-09682-2/$2.95
__LONGARM AND THE MEDICINE WOLF #121	0-515-09875-2/$2.95
__LONGARM AND THE REDWOOD RAIDERS #132	0-515-10193-1/$2.95
__LONGARM AND THE PAWNEE KID #134	0-515-10241-5/$2.95
__LONGARM AND THE DEVIL'S STAGECOACH #135	0-515-10270-9/$2.95
__LONGARM AND THE WYOMING BLOODBATH #136	0-515-10286-5/$2.95
__LONGARM IN THE RED DESERT #137	0-515-10308-X/$2.95
__LONGARM AND THE CROOKED MARSHAL #138	0-515-10334-9/$2.95
__LONGARM AND THE TEXAS RANGERS #139	0-515-10352-7/$2.95
__LONGARM AND THE VIGILANTES #140	0-515-10385-3/$2.95
__LONGARM IN THE OSAGE STRIP #141	0-515-10401-9/$2.95
(On Sale Sept. '90)	

For Visa and MasterCard orders call: 1-800-631-8571

FOR MAIL ORDERS: CHECK BOOK(S). FILL OUT COUPON. SEND TO:

BERKLEY PUBLISHING GROUP
390 Murray Hill Pkwy., Dept. B
East Rutherford, NJ 07073

NAME_____

ADDRESS_____

CITY_____

STATE _____ ZIP _____

PLEASE ALLOW 6 WEEKS FOR DELIVERY.
PRICES ARE SUBJECT TO CHANGE WITHOUT NOTICE.

POSTAGE AND HANDLING:
$1.00 for one book, 25¢ for each additional. Do not exceed $3.50.

BOOK TOTAL	$ _____
POSTAGE & HANDLING	$ _____
APPLICABLE SALES TAX (CA, NJ, NY, PA)	$ _____
TOTAL AMOUNT DUE	$ _____

PAYABLE IN US FUNDS.
(No cash orders accepted.)

201c